THE HONEY TRAP

THE HONEY TRAP

THEA WOLFF

BLOOMSBURY

First published 2004

Copyright © 2004 by Thea Wolff

The moral right of the author
has been asserted

Bloomsbury Publishing Plc, 38 Soho Square,
London W1D 3HB

A CIP catalogue record for this book
is available from the British Library

ISBN 0 7475 7193 7

10 9 8 7 6 5 4 3 2 1

Typeset by Palimpsest Book Production Ltd,
Polmont, Stirlingshire
Printed by Clays Ltd, St Ives plc

All papers used by Bloomsbury Publishing
are natural, recyclable products made from
wood grown in well-managed forests. The
manufacturing processes conform to the
environmental regulations of the country
of origin.

ACKNOWLEDGEMENTS

Huge thanks to everyone at Bloomsbury, especially the truly wonderful Rosemary Davidson, my editor. To Jonny Geller and Doug Kean for your support and guidance. To Paul Blezard, ta for the title. Benedict Flynn and Jack Barth, cheers so for your advice and suggestions. To the following: Augusta Marguez, Sam Katz, Bongi MacDermot, Rachel Fehily, Rachel Khoo, Lynnette Kyme, Sian Jacobs, Ann-Marie Kavanagh, Bethan Williams and Judy Davis, thank you all so very much for your constancy in friendship. The Hampden Ladies, Wendy, Sandra, Bernie, Marcelline, Debbie C., Debbie J. and Susan for the fine care you took of my No. 1 priority. To the class of Amused Mooses Sept 03 (Ha ha). And finally to Michael Seresin – for everything.

To my family – with love and more love.

THE FINGER

It upset me. I have to say the finger upset me. Pointed straight at me, like a sign or something, like the whole of the universe was giving it to me, the finger, that is.

A little finger, a left-hand pinkie.

Gnarled it was, with traces of red varnish.

Straight at me, pointing.

Thing was, the fact of the matter being, it came without a hand, an arm, or a body, and whichever way you look at it, that's kind of freaky.

MEN ON THE VERGE

Sitting in the office manning the 'Hello, hello'. Monday, early evening, green light lit and all stations go.

I coughed to clear my grimy throat, and, 'The Honey Trap, how can I help?'

My caller sounded nervous, hesitant, like she couldn't quite find the right words, though I knew what she was going to say. She was having a trust crisis. As with everyone else who calls the Honey Trap, she basically suspects her other half, a. has had an affair, b. is having an affair, or c. would like to have an affair, and this is exactly what we specialise in, apprehending men on the verge.

How trustworthy is your mate? Exactly how faithful? Can he be tempted? Will he succumb? Invariably the answer is yes, but the question remains: How easily? At the Honey Trap we test the strength of modern-day marriages. The forecast ain't good, and to date the company has successfully instigated seventy divorces. Quite an achievement. Our success rate is up by twenty per cent on last year's score. Since I joined, as a matter of fact.

Sure, we've saved a few marriages, but let's face it: if you're calling us, there's a problem. It's probably just a matter of time, unless of course the client is actually and certifiably crazy. We have had one such woman. In the end we were forced to get a restraining order. A certain Wacko Wilhemina, who didn't even have a husband to begin with, but that's another story.

'It's just . . .' The caller was snivelling, on the brink of tears. 'Things haven't been the same since I had Billy.'

Their second son. I'm privy to much, probably too much.

Marital bliss?

In my opinion a marketing slogan thought up by a gay bloke. And as for *die Kinder* . . . ah children, God bless 'em, but don't they just go and throw a spanner in the works. I understand, having one of my own.

So wifey rings us, near cracking point.

'He's not there for me. I'm doing everything in the home, holding down a full-time job and seeing to the kids. He just doesn't seem to understand. It's so exhausting, he refuses to pull his weight and' (wait for it) 'still expects me to go down on him.'

Nothing untoward so far. I wasn't listening, not really. I was mulling over the finger. It was cut, or rather hacked, the blood dry and crackly.

Max found the finger. I'd sent him out to the garden to calm down after he'd told me he wasn't my friend. He'd got into a rage, having repeatedly flung his favourite video against the wall, only to realise that such actions would, indeed, break it. Sometimes I wonder if he sees me solely as an extension of himself – 'cause he blames me for everything.

'Go away,' he'd screamed at full lung capacity. 'I'm not your friend.'

So there I was, friendless, or at least with one friend fewer than I'd thought, chopping up some apple, and there he was, red in the face, as I'd refused to acknowledge his anger and get pulled in. But he wouldn't let up, so I'd had to open the back door to the garden and push him outside.

'Out, Max, and don't come back till you've calmed down.'

Immediately I'd reached for my karmic calmers, my pack of fags, and smoked two in a row. Outside, Max wailed for five minutes and then went quiet, really quiet, too quiet. By the time I'd stubbed out the second fag the thought had crossed my mind that he'd been abducted. I'd raced out to find him bent over and poking at something.

'Hey, Maxy, what you found?'

Usually it's stuff like worms, slugs, cat shit or ladybirds.

'A finger.'

'Hello . . . you still there?' asked anxious wifey, sensing my preoccupied mind.

'Yeah . . . do you have any evidence?'

I could hear her kids in the background.

'I mean, we're happily married, it's just . . . Ned, please be quiet . . . Ned, Mummy's on the phone.'

My caller was seeking reassurance. She wanted us to reaffirm her and her husband's bond of trust; she needed to know that he couldn't be tempted, that he wouldn't stray. She also wanted her kid who was throwing a tantrum in the background to shut up, 'cause she couldn't hear herself think. She said she'd ring back as soon as she could.

'No problems, but hey, don't leave it too long. It's better to nip these things in the bud,' I, helpful as ever, advised, or rather teased her burgeoning sense of insecurity.

THE OVERCOAT

The door to the office swung open and Charlie/Fiona, my transgender boss, appeared with my current love interest wrapped around her. Bitch/Bastard. How sad to be so obsessed by an inanimate object, but it's sublime. It's a coat. A beautiful, black, three-quarter-length, cashmere-mix, soft and warm, superbly cut, incredibly expensive coat. I liked the coat. Fiona looked good in it, but I'd look better. I wanted that coat.

I want, I want, I want . . . my little Maxim . . . his favourite saying, mantra . . . And you know what? Wouldn't it be awful if one didn't have any desires?

The coat was, unfortunately, beyond my means. I told Fiona straight out that it didn't do much for her, the motive being to make her sell it to me at a knockdown price.

Fiona's tall, with a fine pair of shoulders. First time Maxy met her, he asked why s/he was wearing women's clothes.

Coolly Fiona stated to my toddler, 'I am a woman.'

4

'Nah, you're not,' he grinned, thinking she was being funny.

She wasn't, and Max looked to me for an explanation. The old adage ringing true that nothing compares to the forthright honesty of a child. However, this had occurred during the job interview, and I truly thought Max had blown it for me.

'Does your son have a problem with transgenders?' enquired Fiona.

'Not usually,' I'd replied.

Having hung up the coat, Fiona made towards our cubby hole cum kitchenette, or rather she took one step to her right and then disappeared into what once must have been a built-in closet. The doors have since been removed, allowing for a mini-fridge beneath a counter and a kettle on top. The office was basic: one room on the second floor of a building on Parkway. Below us were accountants, and below them, an optician.

Fiona popped her head around the corner.

'Want a cup of something, Issy?'

I nodded.

'Sure, and how's Charlie today?'

'Fuck off.'

To wind her up I call Fiona Charlie. It's a joke she doesn't want to get. See, at a stretch, the set-up here is pretty much the same as in the seventies TV show, *Charlie's Angels*.

THE HONEY TRAP

Once upon a time there were three very different little girls. They grew up to be three very different women, but they had three things in common. They were all beautiful, all single mothers, and they all worked at the Honey Trap.

First off there's me, Issy, and I'm Kelly 'cause of my brown hair. Next up is Nadia, the aspiring singer. She's been aspiring for ten years, so strictly speaking she's an expiring singer. Nadia is Sabrina, mainly 'cause I don't want to be Sabrina (too serious, too clever by half). And lastly there's Trisha, the blonde one, the 'I may look like a sexy flirty Farrah Fawcett type, but if you mess with me, I'll burst your balls in one single squeeze.' Trisha is strange, a gym freak, and I don't trust her one bit.

We share the common bond of raising our kids without significant others. This is where our Bosley comes in: Maria, a fifty-year-old Spanish granny, who by day is a charlady and by night the babysitter, thus allowing us Honeys to go on our various missions. Everyone likes Maria. Max adores Maria. If you could choose your own mother, you'd want her to be Maria.

Which just leaves Fiona, the big boss. We don't get to see so much of her, what with her impending op. She tends to drop by now and again to check all's working smoothly, though invariably at the wrong time, like when I'm making a personal call to Mexico. I swore to Fiona it was a one-off, but she didn't believe me, checked the phone bill, and docked twenty quid off my wages.

VACANT SITUATIONS (OR HOW I BECAME A HONEY)

So nine months back I found myself in the middle of a vacant situation. Sitting in a dentist's waiting room, waiting, and whilst in this state of limbo I perused the *Camden New Journal* and came across the following: 'The Honey Trap, est. 2000, specialising in marital trust bonds, seeks a certain type of woman.' It was positioned in amongst the personals, which was odd. I found it directly below this assertive little PO box number: 'U, commitment-phobic, co-dependent Oedipal wreck with financial problems? Me, early thirties, work in media, low self-esteem, call now!' Not that I, you understand, would ever consider using such a service, but I do enjoy laughing at the people who do.

I'd read on: 'The Honey Trap is currently looking for women with attitude'. I have attitude, albeit like a stinky French cheese. 'Women who like a challenge . . .' I love challenges. After three years of interrupted sleep, there are times when getting up in the morning is a challenge. 'Attractive women who know how to play the game and get away with it.' On a good day I scrub up well. 'Flexibility a must'. Knew the yoga would come in handy.

In effect this job had my name written all over it. Issy Brodsky, 36 24 36. OK, so in the good old days. OK, so not even then, but following the advice of several self-help manuals on positive thinking this was exactly how I'd learnt to regard my reflection. Why diet when you can lie to yourself? Plus, and here's a good tip for any body-conscious females out there, always try and befriend fatter people than you. Sure, over the years I'll admit I have expanded a little, wear and tear, but I thank Christ that on the birth of Max I didn't suffer from hideous stretch marks, specifically the ones that wriggle upwards. Lucky that, especially seeing as I still had some left over from a pudgy adolescence. I digress, but Jesus, the fallout of pregnancy. If only half of the stuff was common knowledge, I swear it would put women off breeding.

All in all, the position sounded intriguing. I called the number and enquired further on the specific nature of the job. Unbelievably, when I confessed my single-mum status to Fiona, she didn't flinch. This was an unusual reaction – for all the joys of motherhood, it's a restrictive business. One is at the beck and call of another being twenty-four hours a day. I required a job that would take that into account, i.e. in real terms, I could never be wholly relied upon.

'A problem, not,' declared Fiona. 'All my girls are single mums. Come in, we'll have a chat.'

How astonishingly refreshing, and though the thought crossed my mind that the company was an escort agency or something along those lines, it hadn't put me off.

We arranged a time, and I trawled through my wardrobe in search of something befitting an interview situation. My sad wardrobe, so obviously geared towards my status: cheap, worn-out and stained. My clothes had seen better days; guess I'd seen better days. Comfort and endurance were the usual criteria. I reckoned an investment in my future was long overdue, trotted down to the local charity shops, and finally found a short skirt and top that would do the trick.

Let's face it, jobs of real satisfaction are hard to come by for someone in my predicament. A nine to five would mean full-time child care – expensive, and you had to be committed to a type of bureaucracy I had always abhorred. Before I gave birth I'd worked, well, to be frank, as little as possible. I had a degree, a Master's, had done a stint in France (i.e. a year of intense passion with

8

un mec who screwed up my head), worked for a casting agency, a modelling agency, a photographer's agency. On reflection I'd always been an agent of one kind or another. My laissez-faire or fairly lazy attitude meant I wasn't ever in the position of earning large enough stacks to afford a full-time nanny, and my positions were never such that there was a major pull to go back to work. But the desire to do something other than slave to my child had seeded, and I'd begun to cast around at what was on offer.

There really wasn't much.

ONE RULE

At the job interview Fiona put it to me bluntly.

'There's only one rule here: on no account are you ever to sleep with a client's husband. Do you understand?'

'I don't do married men.'

'Why not?'

'Moral reasons,' I replied, then, hoping to support my case, added, 'I'll never forget the look on my mother's face the day she found out about my father's mistress.' (Actually it was one of relief: it later turned out she'd been shagging his best friend.)

Next up I had to assert what I considered to be my qualifying strengths for the position. I stated that of the many men I'd encountered during my life a fair few had called me a prick-tease, basically because I'd refused to sleep with them.

'Interesting,' she replied.

Actually it's rather tedious.

'Do you hate men?'

'On the contrary, I'm fascinated, but to be honest,

9

there's few and far between who I'd ever, well . . . consider an appropriate partner.'

'What are you looking for, Mr Perfect?' she snorted rather condescendingly.

'See the thing is, Fiona . . . I'm not actually looking. I enjoy male company but I guess, what with Max, my time is stretched as it is.'

Hey, and there was absolutely no way I'd be able to deal with a second kid.

'Hmm . . . so do you think you'd be interested in the job?'

'Yeah. Definitely.' Sure would beat working as a supermarket cashier.

'OK, Issy, we'll try you out.'

As interviews go it was easy enough. Max and I celebrated with ice-cream cones from Marine Ices: a double scoop of pistachio and morello cherry for me, and for Max, strawberry with strawberry sauce.

'Max, this is the beginning of something big,' I proclaimed, to which he'd replied, 'More, I want some more.'

'Max,' I continued, 'I love you.'

'I want to do a poo, Mum.'

Ended up having to sprint the buggy home to avoid a minor accident.

SO . . .

Eight months back I joined the Honey Trap and became a special agent of sorts, an agent provocateur, a fidelity barometer, a sticky honey strip (like the yellow ones my Gran hung in her kitchen attracting hosts of summer bluebottles to an early demise – though it must be said, not the most appetising sight when sitting down for a Sunday roast).

Hey, at the end of the day I have a job and a reinforced sense of self-worth. It's amazing what a brown envelope can do. The added bonus being I'm able to get out a couple of times a week with a free babysitter thrown in for good measure. In a nutshell there's enough cash, which, topped up with Child Benefit, lone-working-parent tax relief et al, is enough to keep Max and me bobbing sweet.

SO . . .

Eight months later and Fiona was screaming at me, 'What the fuck is this?'

'What does it look like?'

THE STARTING POINT

'It's a finger,' shouted Max. 'Look, Mummy.'

He'd picked it up and come sprinting over to me. Pointed it at me and said, 'See, it's a finger.'

'Sweet fuck!'

I usually do my best to cut down on the bad language, I swear. OK, so I confess, part of me, the weak-pun part, harbours delusions of being a stand-up comedian. No, really, upon motherhood I have had to amend my vocabulary accordingly.

Max gaped at me strangely, and then from out his rosebud lips there trilled a sing-song tirade of 'Sweet fuck's.

Crouched down by his side I turned a greenish hue, due to the finger, not the foul-mouthed boy child whom I then ignored. At the same time I desperately tried to gulp back a recently digested cheese sandwich that was trampolining on the lining of my stomach.

'Where did you find it?'

I'd shuddered, expecting to see the rest of the body lying in the near distance. Together we searched our pathetic patch of grass with one solitary rose bush, otherwise known as the garden. Thankfully there was nothing, absolutely nothing.

'This is so weird, Max.'

'Sweet fuck, Mum.'

To whom did it belong? Where had it come from, and more importantly, what the hell was it doing in my garden? So many possibilities, though I figured it probably belonged to a kidnap victim. Some poor ultra-wealthy woman was walking around with only four digits. Which meant . . . I would be generously rewarded for finding the missing finger and get my picture in the papers.

In the distance I heard the doorbell buzz and guessed it was Maria.

WHICH MEANT . . .

Time to don my alter ego and go fight the evil forces of potential adultery.

I casually explained all this to Fiona, whose mouth curled at the edge in disbelief.

'Anyhow I thought I'd drop it by a police station on the way, but I was running late so I just popped it into a freezer bag and left it in the fridge.'

Fiona wasn't very sympathetic.

'Issy, it's disgusting. I want the finger removed.'

'It already has been removed. Hacked off, in fact.'

She had no idea how long, and how much effort, it had taken me to get Max to let go of it. All the distractions and clowning about.

'Mine, mine, mine. My finger!' he'd howled, refusing to let go of it.

'Max, you already have ten fingers – one more ain't going to be of any use whatsoever.'

And so I'd had to chase him round the flat for twenty minutes, and then play hide and seek. This gets real boring 'cause Max only has one hiding place, under the covers of my bed.

Fiona was furious.

'Issy, I have a thing about fingers. Can you please get rid of it?'

'Fine, fine. I'll go to the police station right now. That OK?'

Fiona wasn't even meant to be in the office tonight.

'Actually no, I've got a job for you. Trisha's had to pull out of it. I need you to take over.'

'Why?'

'Because it's a case she's been working on for ages and I don't want to blow the account.'

OK, so Trisha is a six-foot-tall, slim, blonde, brassy dominatrix type, and I am none of those things.

'How come she can't do it?'

'Her youngest has a fever. You're going to have to do it.'

Fiona handed me a chipped mug of instant espresso and a case file.

Mr Bob Thornton, thirty-nine, married with two kids. His missis had been poking her nose into his computer and found plenty of virtual adulterous activity.

His method of covering up such dirty doings was to spell his name backwards. Clever that. Trisha, her alias being Trixi, had been communicating with him for the past three weeks, egging him further down the line towards maintenance payments with lascivious emails of the like:

> Dirty Bob, your last email left me soaking, had to take a long shower and scrub hard, was thinking of you all the while. Can't help wanting to meet you for real. Are you really like you say you are? Trixi.

> Trixi, I've been a v. bad boy. Need to be taken in hand and disciplined hard. I dream of you walking all over me with your six-inch heels and long red nails clawing into my hairy back. How big is your mouth?

> Dirty Bob, you disgust me, just the way I like it.

> Trixi, I want to ding-dong you. Let's meet and do it.

Figured I was in for a sophisticated night, not. Bob described himself as: having brown hair (a full head of), a six-footer and looking remarkably young for his age. Thankfully Trisha hadn't mailed him a picture of herself, but it was clear from the emails he was expecting one powerful dame.

'Fiona, I'm not sure I'll get away with this.'

My whole demeanour spelt out nice, gentle woman, not ball-breaker, bitch, emasculator.

Fiona, clicking her knuckles, regarded me with disdain, my skirt too long, my make-up too demure.

'Borrow something from the cupboard.'

The emergency cupboard contained odds and sods of clothing for such situations. I had a rummage and found a short, tight skirt and a pair of high-heeled, knee-length black boots. I swept my hair up off my face into a super-tight ponytail, Sade style, stretching back the skin on my face. Next up I smeared a real generous amount of blood-red on my lips and finished off the look with a false beauty spot.

Time ticking onward, expected in half an hour and I was looking more the part till I put on my puffa jacket. Fiona eagle-eyed me whilst reading out bits and pieces from the file: Bob collects cigarette picture cards. Bob's favourite drink is beer. Bob has a caravan and every summer takes his family camping in France. Bob is a member of a bird watchers' society.

'Oh and Bob likes to shit on his own doorstep.'

Nothing surprises me these days.

'Trixi, you are meeting your date at the Phoenix in Tufnell Park.'

'That's practically at the end of his road.'

'Yeah, a real nice guy. Make sure you get him.'

'Right, guess I best be off.'

Fiona gave me the once-, twice-over.

'The jacket ruins it. You look like a tarted-up market woman.'

'There's nothing else in here.'

'Shit . . . Bob hates tardiness,' Fiona growled. 'Borrow my coat.'

'You sure about that?'

'Yeah, drop it by tomorrow.'

Ushering me out of the office, she handed me some money for expenses.

'Well, what are you waiting for?'

Fiona once threatened me with probation for being. Yeah, for just being. She used to work for the prison service, a guard in a women's prison. She's pre-op and moody as hell.

I jumped to attention and was halfway out the door when she hollered, 'What about the finger?'

'You want me to take the finger with?'

'You're not leaving it here.'

'You want me to carry it in this teensy-weensy excuse for a bag?'

Who invented the clutch bag? So totally useless.

'Fiona, can't I just pick it up on the way home?'

'Issy, you can shove up your arse as far as I'm concerned. Get it out of here.'

Yes, sir! She's a man at heart and there's no getting away from it.

MISSION: TO TAPE BOB IN A NEAR COMPROMISING SITUATION

Sometimes things don't go to plan, no matter how well laid out, and it happened that I was laid out. But back to Parkway. I was feeling flustered, teetering on the kerb in killer high-heels and doing my utmost to blank the whingeing homeless guy.

'No, I don't want a *Big Friggin' Issue*, thanks.'

The sky began gobbing down on me, and I flinched as a string of unlit cabs sailed past. Beautiful coat, though, perhaps a couple of sizes too big, at least two weeks' wages worth of rapidly moistening, cashmere-mix. I ended up getting: drenched, the bus, and squashed by an obese lady.

I'd sprung up screaming, 'An eclipse, an eclipse.'

Fatty then had the audacity to claim she hadn't noticed me, as she lowered her colossal rear in my direction. The bus, now lopsided, chugged its load up towards Tufnell Park. Fifteen minutes later it was time to alight and by luck I found the pub easily enough, chiding myself for splashing in puddles on the way – another bad habit picked up from Max.

It's actually quite good fun, the kick, the splash, the wet water soaking through to your toes. The 'double-footed plunge – jump straight in' is much recommended. One becomes the tossed pebble, OK, so in my case, boulder, but the gesture by its very nature is so defiant. Maybe that's why Max has stopped jumping in puddles, because I never say 'Stop' or 'Don't', thereby sapping the forbidden-pleasure aspect out of it. Or maybe he's already embarrassed by his mother's antics. Jeez, I realise he's way advanced for his age, but to be three-and-nearly-a-half and already hoping his mates won't see me with him . . .

I deviate, but only 'cause I know what comes next.

BOB . . .

I'd love to skip this bit, but as with all humiliating moments in my life, it is these I remember in glorious Technicolor and seem unable to mentally purge.

So the next day . . .

God damn it . . .

The truth?

It was a mistake, a huge, big, horrible nightmare.

Into the Phoenix I'd ventured. The place was a bit of a gastro pub. A happy place, with a smattering of jolly people seemingly having a great time, except for the one in the corner who had a face on her that would curdle milk. A face that unfortunately belonged to me, belying thoughts of, Where the fuck is this jerk? and, Why aren't I out with friends instead of wilfully assisting in the ruin of someone's marriage?

A quick once-over confirmed no one particularly fitting the given description. I ordered a vodka at the bar and observed an underager being politely but forcefully asked to leave. I remember well such humiliations in my teens. If I managed to get past the bouncer, the likelihood of actually purchasing a drink was slim, unless of course someone else went to the bar on my behalf. I'd always aim for the nooks and crannies in which to try and hide my underage self. Poor spod, I mused, watching him being escorted off the premises. If I wasn't working, I probably would have claimed he was my younger cousin and bought him a whisky and Coke.

The Kiwi bar tender asked if I was OK.

'I'm meant to be meeting a guy called Bob.'

'Cool. Do you want another drink?'

Second drink purchased, a whisky and Coke. I returned to the corner stool and watched the clock, hoping Bob wouldn't show, that he had bottled it and I could go home. By law, Fiona's, that is, we give the guy an hour tops. Personally it's fifteen minutes – he had ten minutes left.

'Excuse me.'

Tappity tap on my shoulder and oh, let's see, who could it be? Enter one very dirty Bob.

'Bob?'

'Yeah.'

'Hi, I'm Trixi.'

Not too hideous, pleasantly surprised by his boy-next-door look. Six-footer? My arse. Still, a couple more drinks and we'd be talking Hugh Grant-ish.

So we got chatting: blah, blah, blah, a few drinks, ha,

ha, ha, more drinks, yawn, ha, blah and then we ended up fucking.

EXCUSE ME!

The next morning I lay in bed beside a two-foot male. Max easing my eyelids open with his fingers. Daylight forced in like shards of glass, straight at the pupils. My head heavy and breath rank. Peeled myself off the covers, rose up to a sitting position, mind slowly catching up, but my conscience already on at me.

Oh my God, I didn't, I did, didn't, did.

Didn't.

Did.

What the hell had happened? How could I?

Had I been drugged by a near stranger? I wished, but unfortunately, no. It was of my own accord and free will that I found my knickers swimming round my ankles and myself willingly partaking in carnal relations with Bob.

Excuses: one vodka, three whiskies, two tequilas and all on an empty stomach. No, that really won't do. OK, so I was caught mid-cycle, doubling the effects of any alcohol consumption, and my physical being practically baying at the moon for what it must, by the laws of nature, attain.

Poppycock!

It's true, I swear on my life.

I was drunk and desperate and shit happens.

So where did it happen?

Is it really necessary to know all the details?

Spit it out.

What – the exact circumstances under which I found myself in his car?

HIS CAR?

Yeah, like when I was young(er) and carefree. Oh Christ, I tried to reason with my conscience. It wasn't all my fault. Surely he was plastered too? Besides, I'd closed my eyes when it was happening.

But it *did* happen and I'd broken the rule. 'The rule, the rule,' echoed my conscience, then added for good measure, 'You're so completely fucked.'

I'd fled the scene of the crime and caught a cab home. It was 3 a.m. when I arrived. Maria was really pissed off.

'What happened?' she cried, as I tumbled into the hall-way, displaying some drunk stunt action and tripping up on my heels.

Bleary-eyed, I'd managed to mumble, 'Shorry, shorry,' then hurled myself through my bedroom door, collapsed in a heap on the bed and watched the four corners of my room spin.

'Here . . . Issy, some water.'

Maria had followed me into the bedroom with a large glass of water, a bucket, and several Paracetamol.

'Issy, you be OK?'

'Bysee bye.'

Eyelids closed, opened, closed, opened.

Morning already.

'Stop, Max. Please. Mummy has a sore head,' and him jumping for joy at the sight of a new day.

The enthusiasm of youth, the boundless energy that he has, in sharp contrast to my own, lack of, and up on my bed, bouncity bounce.

I was sick as a dog, yet managed to get every drop in the bucket. Next up? A shower. Felt a smidgen better, ready for painkillers, two please, no, make it three, and all washed down with extra-strong black coffee.

It was by then eight-thirty, and I felt a. very delicate

and b. extreme guilt, as I'd barely managed to say a word to Max, having only the capacity to grunt, and shake some Rice Krispies into his bowl.

Fresh air would help. I managed to cart Max down to the nursery, growl a pathetic, 'Later,' about-turn, shuffle home, and make it back to the cistern-leveller for some good old heave-ho.

And then it hit me. My mind near paralysed by the realisation that I'd put my job on the line for a Bob.

FOR A SHAG

A mucky fumble. Come closing time we'd tumbled out of the pub and for some reason I was laughing. Oh yeah, that was it, Bob had actually stumbled and I thought this hysterical. Back on his feet, he brushed himself down and then, half joking, sort of pushed me up against the brick wall and . . .

My lips, swollen, were flooded by such warm feelings. Hey, I'm referring to my facial lips. I hadn't been kissed in a long while. Lip suckered, ah what joy. His pressed against mine, hands clasped around my face, mine around his waist, and I pulled him in close. Impassioned or desperate? The latter if I'm honest. Whatever, it happened and he, the thing was . . . he was a great kisser. Gobalicious. Up against the wall, we shuffled round a bit.

Then . . .

'Where you going?' I gasped, as his suction pads left mine.

'My car.'

'You can't drive in this shtate.'

'Want to get my bag, live around the corner.'

Well, it happened sort of quickly and by then it was too late, the damage done.

I'd followed him to his car, to the back seat. Jesus, I needed it bad – been watching too many episodes of *Sex and the City*.

'This really, really, really, shouldn't have happened,' I shlurred.

'Trixi. That your real name?'

'No.'

WISHING ON MIRACLES

In the light of day, the next day, having dropped Max off and emptied my stomach, in reverse, I sank back on to my bed. There was no way I'd be able to keep my job. This indiscretion was, after all, a major balls-up. In every way, I was screwed. I resorted to religion and prayed.

Dear Lord,
I know I haven't believed in you since I found out fairies didn't exist, and that my imaginary friend was merely a voice in my head, but in my hour of need, please, I beg you, please don't let me lose my job over this minor blip. You see, my job, well, to be honest, it's the only sane thing in my life at the moment. So I'd really appreciate it if you were able to provide some sort of minor miracle on my behalf. God, please don't let anyone at the office find out I slept with Bob. Please?

Are you there, God?

Look, I know it was a truly stupid thing to do.

God?

Hey, it's not like I'm asking for world peace or anything, just a tiny favour. I really love this job, it's a buzz and gets me out, and I swear to you in the future I'll be more charitable. I'm depending on you.

Thanks, yours sincerely,

Issy Brodsky.

HANGOVER REMEDY

Is there such a thing? I slept for the next couple of hours. Felt even worse when I woke, glanced at the time, and realised I'd ten minutes to get to the nursery, a fifteen-minute walk away. Christ, Max would be the last child to be picked up. In mother-speak we're talking massive psychological damage here. So I ran or more like heaved myself down the street. Puff, pant, retch, reaching my destination only to find I'd misread the tick-tock. Phew for Max, but it left me with an hour of fretting.

I was doomed, whatever way I chose to look at my situation. Fucking Bob was not a good idea. By rights I should have already called the office and reported on last night's activities. Instead, I prevaricated in a café, mulling over a coffee and a Danish pastry. My body could no longer take such abuse. Time was, I could have partied for forty-eight hours flat out, but that was before Max, prior to sleep-deprivation and the shackles of motherhood. What in the name of God was I going to say to Fiona? Then there was the coat, Fiona's lovely coat, last seen in a heap on my bedroom floor. Shit, and I hoped it wouldn't require dry-cleaning.

Had I done a Lewinsky? Poor Monica, my heart goes out to her. I mean what an idiot, so smitten and then globally shamed. How bizarre that a large percentage of the international community is aware that she had a cigar stuck up her fanny by the President of the United States of America. What a legacy: imagine telling your grandchildren that. It must be costing her thousands in shrink fees. How in the name of Western civilisation has it come to the point whereby we, the public, have a right to know of such graphic details? Two coffees and two Danish pastries later, I was almost functioning again and went to pick up the love bundle.

MAKE MY DAY

The best part of every day is, undoubtedly, arriving at the nursery and seeing Max's little face light up with excitement: 'Mummy, Mummy . . .' It's kinda phenomenal the love they give and it's totally unconditional, even when you're in the most shitty of foul moods.

'Hey, Maxy.'

He threw himself into my arms and slobbered all over my face.

'You have a good day?' I asked.

'David hit me, I said not nice and . . .' A stream of babbling half-sense flowed out.

I put on his jacket, wrapped him up warm, and home we strolled.

Max is a beautiful child, always has been. Sure I'm biased, but the amount of attention elicited from passers-by sticking their faces into the buggy bears this out. I thank my lucky stars he wasn't a grosser, and believe me, I've seen many. The power of maternal love being such that no matter how ugly your offspring, you are blind to it.

Back at the apartment I picked up the coat, gave it a good shake, emptied the pockets, and found the bus ticket with Bob's number scrawled on it (reckon he liked me, a tad). Chucked it out with the rubbish. All evidence must be eradicated. To all intents and purposes, what happened actually did not happen. Hey, an alibi was forming. From the murky depths of my mind I realised exactly what had to be done. Deny everything in order to keep my job. Simple yet perfect. It would be fine, I would trust to faith, and feeling brave I called the office.

Trisha answered.

'All right, Issy?'

'Fine, how's Alice?'

'Aw, it was just a tummy bug.'

'Yeah? I'm not feeling too well myself.'

'I think it's going round.'

Trisha, a divorcee in her late thirties with three kids, spends most of her day ferrying her kids from their various schools to their extra-curricular activities. I can't make her out at all – she's terribly closed. Don't get me wrong, there's nothing nasty about her, it's just we've never actually had a real conversation. You know, like when you trade personal information and talk about feelings. She'll natter about her gym classes, hair dyes, a skirt she saw and tanning sessions, but that's about it.

A few weeks back we were down in a city bar, checking out a wayward hubby who preferred 'working late' to family life. Within half an hour Trisha had him in the palm of her hand, whilst I acted the accomplice. She was brilliant, managed to tape him denying he was married, declaring his desire to bang her and that he would wait outside for her. We left through another exit. As it was only seven-thirty, I asked Trisha if she wanted to go and do something.

'Like what?'

'Like watch a movie or have a drink?'

'Nah fanks . . . got things to do.'

'It's just as Maria's babysitting I thought I could nab a couple more hours.'

'Oh really?'

Off she trotted and I ended up going to see a film on my own. Bad move actually – it was a fanny flick, i.e. a light romantic comedy for the ladies. A perfect date movie, the place full of couples, and I felt incredibly conspicuous.

Ho hum, but worse was to come.

Fiona called me the very next day and said in the most patronising of tones. 'Issy, I know it can be hard being a single mum, but please don't confuse working hours with your social life.'

This comment had me gurning: it hurt 'cause it was sort of true. Anyhow, Trisha, the snitch bitch, had obviously blown the whistle on me. Been wary of her ever since, and to be frank, I was shitting a brick hoping that she, now on the other end of the receiver, wouldn't be able to see through my bare-faced lying.

I gulped back the truth and hastily explained, 'Yeah, Trisha, just calling in to let you know what happened last night.'

So far so good.

'Fiona mentioned you did Bob. How'd it go?'

Oh Christ . . .

'Good. I mean . . . He never showed up.'

Easy, how easy was that?

But would she buy it?

'Really?'

26

The tone of her voice indicated no.

'Yeah, really.' I stressed the 'really'. 'I waited there over an hour and a half.'

There followed a long silent pause. I was sweating. After all it was her case to begin with and you can get pretty possessive over your cases, especially the big ones.

'You saying it was a *no show*?'

'Yeah. A no show. I waited an hour then left.'

'Oh that's strange, 'cause Maria said you never got in till 3 a.m.'

'Well . . . that's sort of why I'm calling in so late today. Bob never showed, but then I' – think, think – 'I bumped into an old friend, from way back, you don't know him, college days, and we just got talking. You know how it is?'

My explanation was met by a stony silence.

I know what I don't like about Trisha: she's a fucking cow, interrogating me like she was my superior or something.

'Don't worry, Trisha, I'll pay for the extra baby-sitting.'

'Right then . . . So I'll put down one hour on your work sheet?'

'Well, I was there an hour and a half, but fine.'

So not fine. I needed the money and who the fuck was she to complete my work sheet?

'Oh and one more fing, Issy. Fiona said you borrowed 'er coat. She wants it back, asap.'

'Sure, I'll drop it over. In the next hour or so, would that suit?'

I'd lied through my teeth, though the ordeal was far from over. Bob's wife would be called and then it was a case of her word against mine. If she said Bob was out on Monday night, which of course he was, suspicions would be raised, and considering I stayed out to 3 a.m., my position didn't look good.

I was so doomed.

25 MINUTES LATER

Still doomed and doing the utmost to ward off a tantrum. Max found it really amusing to watch as my clenched fists pounded my pillows in exasperation. Finally managed to gather myself together.

'OK, Maxy, time to go.'

'No, it's late.'

Now, the thing most kiddie winkies thrive on is routine, and no matter how laid-back one is initially, by the end of the first year a routine of sorts evolves and, before you know it, you are planning your days around them. Basically Max was well peeved when I suggested a walk to the office.

'Sorry, kid, know you're tired, but I have to do this and you're too young to be left alone.'

I bundled him up and off we set.

'Hello, Trisha?'

I buzzed the intercom, hoping I wouldn't have to lug the buggy and Max up three flights of stairs.

'Trisha, it's me. I'm downstairs with Max. You wouldn't do us a favour and run down? I've got Fiona's coat.'

'Give me five minutes.'

Ten in reality. She was really winding me up. And it was freezing. I acted overly grateful when she arrived, smarming at her generosity of spirit that she should venture down three flights.

'Hi, sweetie,' she clucked at Max.

'Thanks, Trisha – it's such an ordeal with the buggy. You know how it is.'

'Issy, word of advice. Between you and me, you'd better toe the line. Fiona's getting pissed off.'

I swear I couldn't say anything. I was choking on a response that never quite made it. I bit my tongue. It rankled and hurt (my tongue, that is). Just 'cause she'd been working there the longest. It gnawed at me, making my lips purse and eyes glower. She was jealous – probably fancied Bob. Yeah, come to think of it, their communications went way beyond the bounds of professionalism. I should take another look in that Bob file. I even considered calling Nadia for a conspiratorial chat.

HOMEWARD BOUND TAKE TWO

Cranky, AKA Max, was distracted by a made-up monster story. 'Trisha the Troglodyte'. Oh, don't you know it? Trisha is a very stupid troglodyte who comes to a horrible, twisted demise when her tongue, under the spell of the good witch Issy, begins to grow longer and longer, and in the end strangles Trisha. This twisted tale took us halfway home, then we spotted several diggers, which never fail to excite, and finally had a minor dispute about whether or not Max was allowed to have an ice-cream. This being the dead of winter. He won, but we made it back.

The evening rituals thus began. Fixed Max his tea, then played his favourite game of the moment, 'traffic jams'. I swear, he lines up his cars one behind the other and shouts, 'Beep, beep,' and, 'Get a move on,' stuff like that. Of course, it all ends in an awful crash. Next up, bath time, with a scrub-a-dub here, a rub-a-dub there, and an unholy mess in the bathroom. This is followed by a video, one I've seen a billion times before. I now know large portions of script from several Disney classics. And finally, finally, a story . . . oops, almost forgot to brush Max's teeth.

'OK, one more story. No, you can't have any more milk. It's time for bed now. Go to sleep, Maxy.' More cuddles, kisses, kisses, 'I love you,' and eventually he goes to sleep.

Time to tidy the flat.

Time to collapse.

I really should ring some people, I thought, old friends who by now are mere acquaintances, just to tell them I'm still alive; but as I haven't kept in touch, it always seems like too much of an effort. Besides I was whacked. Indeed, since Max arrived, I exist on the precipice of exhaustion. It's a drip, drip factor of continuous tiredness from which there is no escape, no respite, and a good night's sleep becomes a luxury. Christ, but how I look forward to putting my head on the pillow of an evening and escaping into the vast dreamland that has become my social world.

But, just as I closed my eyes, a zillion thoughts rushed at me. All the stuff I forgot to do, should have done, things to remember. Bob! It was fun, it offloaded many months of frustration, and yes, I was aching for it. But you know what? There was really no point guilting myself out about it, wagging the finger at myself.

OH SHIT

I forgot – it clean slipped my addled mind. Head on the pillow and surrendering to the peaceful night, when thoughts of the finger struck. Specifically, exactly where I'd left it. Rewound to Fiona telling me where I could stick it and I recalled taking it from the fridge. It was in a freezer bag, wrapped in Cellophane, in my hand and . . . Yes, I'd put it in the coat pocket. I shoved it in the pocket, 'cause it wouldn't fit in the clutch bag, along with my keys, phone and fags. Fuck. It was in the coat that was now back in the office.

'But wait!' My irritating Inner-know-it-all pokes my near-somnolent self and whispers, 'You checked the pockets today, remember?'

Oh yeah, so I had, when I'd chucked out Bob's number.

'And nothing else.'

'What are you trying to say?'

'Nothing . . .'

So if it wasn't in the coat, then . . . Got it, must have put it in my bag, may well have, couldn't recall, but likely, I'd check the bag in the morning.

'No, do it now.'

'No, I need to sleep.'

'Won't let you, I'll play on you.'

I've always talked to myself. It's not a problem as such, though I suppose it's a bit strange. I usually disguise it by pretending I'm talking into my mobile. Works a treat.

'Check the bag now,' urged Inner-know-it-all.

'Tomorrow. I want to go to sleep.'

This went on a fair while, till Know-it-all who knows me so well said, 'Why make such a big deal out of it? You're going to have to get up and pee.'

'What?' (I pressed my bladder: a dribble, if that.) But of course once the idea was planted I had to put on the light and drag myself to the bathroom. I emptied my bag. *Nada*. Fret befell, and I was back up and in the kitchen, making a cup of tea and anxiously smoking a fag.

Reality was sinking in.

I'd lost the finger.

I'd actually lost the finger.

Or had I merely misplaced it?

How could I be so stupid? No smart-arse comments.

OK, so the likelihood was, the finger had fallen out of the coat.

I checked my bedroom, then the whole apartment.

GNAWED NAILS AND DIRTY GREAT BLACK BAGS HANGING OFF MY FACE

The very next day, Wednesday.

'I'd like to report a missing finger.'

In the police station and I was feeling guilty.

'Pardon me?' asked the cute copper, licking the nib of his pencil, eager to take down my particulars.

The missing finger and how I came to lose it? I'd ruminated on this question all night. Well, it could have happened at any point of the said evening: standing out on Parkway, the bus journey up to the pub, in the pub, the thrusting session outside the pub, the shag in the car, or even in the minicab on the way home.

'You found a finger and then lost it?'

'Precisely.'

'It wasn't your finger, by any chance?'

I wagged my ten digits at him, tempted to parley awhile and tell of the time I sliced the tip of my own off, and being in such a rush just stuck it back on with a plaster, hoping for the best, and as luck would have it, it stuck.

'No, my son found it in the garden.'

'How old is your son?'

'Three and a half. Almost.'

'A real finger?'

Does he think I'm crazy?

'Yes, a finger, a little finger, belonging to a female of advanced years.'

'You mean you found a finger?'

'What have I been saying for the past five minutes?'

'And this was a couple of days ago?'

'Like I said, I'm a single mum (my excuse for everything). Look, I found it five minutes before I had to dash out of the house and go to work. I'd intended to report it immediately but due to . . . demands of work I couldn't, and it was only when I returned home I realised I'd lost it.'

'Why didn't you report it missing on Tuesday?'

'See, what happened was, I forgot all about it and it wasn't until Tuesday night that I remembered.'

'You blanked out the fact that you'd found a finger.'

'Look, my job was on the line. I'd got dreadfully drunk on Monday, was sick as a dog, and it was just hideous,' I blurted.

'What was hideous?'

'The hangover. I was panicking like a headless chicken, dealing with Max, and then I had to get the coat back and then, well, see, I made a mistake.'

'What type of mistake?'

'A repercussive one.'

'What? You mean you keep making the same mistake over and over again.'

'No, that's like behavioural patterns. I'm talking about a mistake that could cost me my job.'

'What?'

'I broke the rule.'

'You've lost me.'

'And the finger.'

Before going to the police station, I'd spent much of

the morning retracing my steps of the fateful night. I'd called the Phoenix. The landlord of the pub plainly thought I was a crank, or someone from a TV show, calling in to make a fool out of him. Public humiliation in the name of entertainment. Is humiliation a virtue? I just don't get it. Video clips sent in by people who force their kids, partners and pets to fall or trip, or bang their heads in the most obvious of set-ups, and all for a measly fifty quid. Three in a boat and guess what? They fall into the water. Wow, couldn't see that coming! Ooops, the hose has gone awry and near drowned the baby, or Dad looks like he's doing a massive piss . . . hilarious. Clumsy me, tossing pancakes, and wait for it . . . plop, it fell on my head! Hey, watch out! There's a glass door in front of you . . . oh too late!

I called the minicab company. Unbelievably, the driver in question had ceased to exist. I guess they must have assumed I was some sort of Customs official checking out his status. I called the bus company, was kept on hold for twenty minutes, and then a recorded message informed me I should write in, assuring me that eighty-five per cent of complaints are answered within three to four weeks.

'Look.' I leant in close to the policeman, a young guy, and I was struck hard by the fact I was no longer a young woman. For so long the feared and dreaded law had always been older than me. How things change: before you know it, you're looking middle-age right in the face, and the face is worn-out, eyes heavy, and there is no hint of laughter behind those windows to the soul. The glow of youth has long since been extinguished, and you take to wearing make-up and looking at old photos thinking, Christ, what have I become?

'Look, young man,' snapped I, to the police boy,

attempting to be assertive, though I have joined the ranks of the crippled. Yes, I believe motherhood is a state of near crippledom. One's pace is slowed down and one gets special seats on buses.

'Look, I found a finger, and that's odd. I mean, someone is going round with a missing finger. I think it should be investigated.'

'But you see, Mrs . . .'

'Ms,' I correct him.

'Ms . . . sorry, what is your surname?'

'Brodsky, Isabel Brodsky.'

A QUICK PERSONAL HISTORY

Isabel Brodsky. Born in the last century, a child of the seventies. Irish mother, a lapsed Catholic, Swiss father, a lapsed Jew, and together they made two secular babies. Me and my older brother, Freddie. My mother, a feminist hippy, found herself with two small kids, and an idealistic husband, forced to embrace capitalist ideology and set up a successful marketing business. Pretty soon after that they split, though to be fair to them, it wasn't acrimonious.

I had an easy childhood, stable, loving, and spending time with Dad meant we got to go on loads of holidays. My mum now lives in New Mexico. My father remarried, and lives in Switzerland with his second wife and two kids.

But back to me – at the age of twenty-seven, having missed three periods, I decided to take a test. Lo and behold it proved positive. The donor – for alas, that is all I can call him – I'd met at a music festival and haven't seen since. Two days of joviality, of drugs and wild abandon. Has to be said he was a great lay. Anyhow, we were only ever on first-name terms, but if I saw him again, I'm sure I'd recognise him. I have this image in my head, which is probably a wild distortion of reality, of an incredibly good-looking guy, and Dutch to boot. I think his name was Jan something-or-other. I did of course put little personal ads in *Time Out* and its Dutch equivalent, stuff like, *Jan, met you at Glastonbury, now pregnant, will need child support*. But weirdly I never got a reply.

To make matters worse I was in a long-term relationship at the time. We were coming up to our first anniversary and Finn was away in the rainforest, helping some charity with botanical stuff. He didn't feel like sticking around. Strange that, hey? What you sow, so shall ye reap, or weep in my case. So I found myself forced into taking responsibility for my actions. *Et voilà*, Max.

Wonderful, beautiful, astonishing Max, catapulting me into a world I'd never envisaged. A world I call Heavell. For motherhood has turned out to be a strange state, indeed a mixture of heaven and hell where there is no limbo. Yet for all my griping, I wouldn't want to be anywhere else.

'So, what happens now?' I asked the PC.

'Usual police procedure. I'll pass this information on to my superiors, cross-check with other stations, hospitals, see if it fits with anything.'

'Are you taking me seriously?'

'Very.'

'Promise?'

'Miss Brodsky . . .'

I wondered if he had a girlfriend, if it was opportune to flirt, if a dismembered body lay scattered in amongst the gardens where I lived. Can someone die from a chopped-off finger? Had some old lady bled to death while I, inebriated, needlessly abandoned myself?

Guilt, awash with, and ...

TIME FOR A MIDWEEK CRISIS!

Actions taken had afforded me some relief, yet I remained anxious over work, wondering whether I'd be back on the breadline. I fretted about this all the way to the office. Surely they would have found out that Bob had in fact shown up.

By chance, neither Trisha nor Fiona were at the office. In their stead I found Nadia manning the Trap. I didn't mention the Bob episode, concentrating on the digit dilemma. Nadia listened, enthralled, her mouth agape.

'That is way creepy.'

'Tell me about it – the guy looked so young, it was like confessing to a Boy Scout.'

'How could you do it?'

'What?'

'Lose the finger.'

I felt wretched. Nadia is young. Everyone younger than me I now consider to be young. She had her first kid when she was eighteen, second when she was twenty. Twenty-seven now, she lives with her mum and has this extended-family thing going on, i.e. lots of support. Plus she's doing a part-time degree at the Royal Academy of Music and sings in a band. In mummyspeak, she's a jammy cow. Oh yeah, she is also phenomenally beautiful, in a phwoar-to-almost-scary way. Plus, she's got this really positive attitude and is incredibly easygoing.

I did my best to resist liking her for a long time. Caved

in when I found an envelope she had left for me on the desk containing three rolled-up joints and a note saying, 'Issy, you are giving yourself unnecessary facial lines. Please smoke these and lighten up.'

Max and I hang out with her some weekends, which is fun. In fact, I won't have a word said against her and my envy is restricted to premenstrual-tension days only, which she, bless her, fully understands. See, working together means we have synchronised, allowing us to indulge in the most fantastic bitching sessions and then a few days later make up, when the release flow occurs.

'Nadia, are you so thick as to think I would have lost the finger on purpose?'

'Some old lady bled to death and you did nothing about it.'

'I can't hear you.'

Ears plugged with fingers, another Maxim I indulge in from time to time.

'Issy! A little old dear, so weak she had to fling her own finger out the window of her flat, in a cry for help, and you . . .'

'OK, now you're just being over-dramatic.'

'You'd think someone on your street would have noticed something. You really should ask your neighbours.'

'Talk to my neighbours? Are you crazy?'

In this day and age, one never can be sure who or what one is living next to. As far as I'm concerned, neighbours are people to be avoided at all costs, except if their washing machine has leaked and you need the name of their insurance company to make a claim.

THE MAN ABOVE ME

So there I was, screaming at my neighbour, full throttle enraged, my period expected in less than twenty-four hours. After I'd finished my rat-a-tat-tatting, he, arsehole supremo, squinted his eyes, ignored my question about weird goings-on, and asked, 'Can you ask your kid to keep the noise down?'

Well, that just friggin' did it.

'He's a three-and-a-half-year-old, you fucking jerk, and it's only four o'clock in the afternoon. How dare you.'

'Got a migraine.'

He pointed to his temple.

This is the guy who plays music at eleven o'clock at night (late in mother time), who has baths at midnight, and once turned on his washing machine at 2 a.m.

When he moved in last year, I'd been optimistic. Nice-looking guy, thought we could be friendly. How deceptive appearances can be. I distinctly recall being laden down one afternoon, what with shopping bags and Max, inching towards the front door, in dire need of assistance. Then as I fumbled in my pockets for my keys, all fingers and thumbs, the door opened, he exited, and let it slam shut, like practically in my face, before I could wedge Max in as a doorstop.

'Thanks,' I'd hollered.

'What?' he'd replied.

'You could have let me in.'

'You have your own keys.'

Arghhh, and that marked the beginning of our many run-ins. We now do our best to ignore each other.

My neighbour from hell was telling *me* to keep the noise down.

Me. Christ, I'd only knocked to see if he'd noticed any weirdness of late.

'So if you wouldn't mind, my head is really sore.'

I glowered straight at him, whispering under my breath, 'Here's hoping it's a brain haemorrhage.'

For the next hour, Max and I indulged in a very simple game called, 'Who can scream the loudest.' OK, I confess, Max has brought out the child in me, the spoilt-brat one.

Next day I called the police station to check if they'd found a match yet: they hadn't.

BACK ON THE NIGHT SHIFT

It was Thursday and I was on the night shift. Maria arrived to a rapturous reception from Max. Then, as always, she produced a treat from her jacket pocket, and the next ten minutes were mine to shower and get ready.

'Issy, are you OK?'

'Sure, Maria, why d'you ask?'

'But what happen Monday?'

I hadn't splurged to anyone of my recent nocturnal activities, not even Joy, my closest, dearest friend. Joy decided to go travelling last year (bitch). She'd worked her arse off in the City as a broker, which led to a stress-related illness, which, coupled with her biological clock and no takers, provoked her into handing in her resignation and running off to South America. She hasn't been seen since. I miss her sorely. It actually hurts. We text regularly, since Fiona got wise to my telephone antics, but it's not the same. Of all my friends, I was the first to bairn-produce, and it's taken a while to find a whole new set of kid-friendly people.

'But what happen, Issy? You were in a bad state.' Maria's tone of voice impressing upon me to open up.

Can't pretend any more. Swept too much under the carpet. It's knee-high with emotional debris.

'I . . . I . . . well, Maria, I sorta, kinda, I think I've fucked up badly. Tonight may be my last night on the job.'

I could have brave-faced it, pretended to Maria that all was under control and I'd just pushed the boat out a little too far. Fact was, I was drowning, and what happened that night was a result of pure, unadulterated, triple-x loneliness.

'Maria, you know the one rule at the Trap, the cardinal sin, the boundary not to be crossed . . .'

'I get picture.'

She sighed heavily with genuine concern and then did the wrong thing by putting her arms round me and giving me a hug.

I surprised myself and dissolved into sobs.

'It just gets so lonely looking after Max on my own, and sometimes I need to be held, you know, just held.'

So Maria held me for fifteen minutes, and OK, she wasn't hunk of the month but it was something, and for fifteen minutes it felt like someone was taking care of me, loving me.

I arrived at the office late. Trisha was there waiting for me to take over.

'Sorry I'm late, Trisha. I'll make it up or you can dock my wages.'

'No problem, Issy, the kettle's just boiled. You want a cup of tea?'

What was with the personality makeover? Maria must have rung her.

'Issy, you should go to the gym – it's really good for releasing endorphins.'

'Oh right, thanks.'

Blu-tacked to the noticeboard was a piece of paper with the words 'Don't Abuse Office Time' printed in bold, and for my benefit, no doubt.

'Look, Trisha, I'm really sorry about Monday.'

'Stop apologising. Listen to this, about Bob Thornton . . .'

'Bob?'

Here it comes. I took a deep breath and thought, Whatever happens, it's going to be OK, it's going to fine.

'The thing is, I called Mrs Thornton and she said her husband had gone out on Monday . . .'

So that was why she was being nice – the lead-up to my P45. She was going to string me out to dry – oh twist the knife a little deeper, honey.

'Trisha, I was there. I swear he didn't show up. I'm not lying.'

Scarlet lady, red in the face from deceit.

'I know, I received an email from Bob apologising for Monday night and wanting to meet up again.'

LORD, YOU HEARD MY PRAYER LETTER AND THANK YOU, ALMIGHTYNESS

Off the hook but confused nonetheless. Relief washed away a week of intense anxiety. And you know what? I came on immediately.

'I was thinking you should meet Bob again,' Trisha continued.

'What? No way. You do it, he was your lead originally.'

She handed me a printout of the email: 'Trixi bella belle, Monday was a fuck-up, can we meet up soon, was wondering if you like gigs?'

'That's weird,' I blurted. The whole tone had shifted. 'What's gig shorthand for – some sexual perversion?'

'No, a band playing in a pub.'

'Duh, there I was thinking horse and trap clap, spank as in hanky panky.'

'Issy, stop fussing. Email him back and set up another date.'

'Why me?'

'I have a feeling he was there.'

And before I could say anything to further incriminate myself, Trisha winked at me.

'I think he took one look at you and bottled it. I mean it in a nice way.'

She left a couple of minutes later, off to seek out a certain Roger. He claimed to be a member of a book club. However, his wife's suspicions had been aroused as all the books he'd supposedly read had creaseless spines. A dead give-away, if ever there was one.

I fixated on thoughts of Bob. Was he some mighty game player? Did he know his wife read his emails? Were they actually perverts and having some warpo fun? It didn't add up: there was something awry.

I sent an email to him, kept it vague: 'Dirty Bob, Monday was indeed a fuck-up, I'll give you one last chance to make it up to me. Trixi, tricksy belle.'

TING-A-LING-A-LING-A-LING

The green light gloweth, arm in action and . . .

'Good evening, the Honey Trap. How can I help?'

'Hello? Hello? Is anyone there?' A Yiddisha mama speaketh.

'Hi, the Honey Trap.'

'Can you talk up a little louder, I haven't got my hearing aid in.'

I wind the volume up.

'Hello. The. Honey. Trap.'

'Can you hear me?'

A shrill old dear was piercing my eardrums.

Suddenly it dawned: was this the woman with the missing finger? Could it be? Could it possibly be . . . ?

'Are you . . .'

'Finklestein,' she said.

'Yes, but is this about the finger?'

'Finkle . . . as in F.I.N.K.L.E.S.T.E.I.N. Look, you can . . .'

CALL ME GLADYS

Oi, Gladys, but did she go on some. I'm paid to listen – that's what I kept saying to myself over and over.

'He's not himself. I don't know what it is, but to be honest these last couple of weeks something's changed. He's lost his umph, you know what I mean?'

'Umm . . .' To be honest I didn't.

'Not umm . . . umph. He was always so full of it and now . . .'

'How old is he?'

44

'Seventy-nine.'

'I see, and you think he could be having an affair?'

'After fifty years of marriage you think I care . . . I know this isn't strictly what your company is for, but look . . . Can you talk to him? Get some sense out of him? Make him smile, though not too much – he's just had a heart-bypass operation. What colour hair do you have?'

'Brown.'

'You a nice girl? Educated?'

'Yeah . . .'

'Think you could help me out?'

'Excuse me for being naive, but why don't you use an escort company?'

'Have you seen how much they charge? Listen, he needs a bit of attention from a stranger, a total stranger . . . see what I'm saying?'

'It's not really our thing, Mrs Fink.'

'From one woman to another . . . please . . . please . . . I'm at my wits' end. Just the once. Please?'

'OK, I'll see what I can do.'

'So every second Monday, he goes to Harry's after work – you like chicken soup? They do good chicken soup . . .'

A DATE SET FOR MONDAY

Me and the boy child got through the weekend, the pair of us gagging come Monday morning for some quality separation time. He flew out of my arms, screaming the name of his best friend of the moment, without a kiss goodbye, not even a wave ta-ta. I turned and went to hang his coat on his name peg. Left the nursery and –

Yes! Freedom, Monday. MY DAY. Reserved for doing things I wanted to do.

Like read the Sunday papers, like call someone and have an uninterrupted telephone conversation, go see an early-afternoon movie, go to the gym, have lunch with a friend, but first I must settle bills, clean the apartment, wash a week's worth of laundry, consult the list of things to be fixed and decide to do it another day, plan the week, the weekend, counter-plan, un-plan, update wish lists, daydream on what ifs, check my insurance, and just as I sit down with my coffee ready to open the papers, it's time to collect Max.

My big date with Mr Joel Finklestein was planned for that very evening. Fiona didn't care that it wasn't strictly kosher, just as long as she got paid. I was slightly anxious about it. I mean how the hell do you go about flirting with an elderly man?

'YO, DIG THE TURKEY WATTLE!'

Joel Finklestein had shrunk with age. A slight man in a dark-grey suit, with silver hair, watery eyes sunk back in his face, and hand slightly shaking as he raised the soup spoon to his mouth. He was staring out the large front window of the restaurant on to the high street. Harry Morgan's, St John's Wood, a comfort-food haven.

The place was near empty when I arrived. I sat at the table next to him, my opening gambit a weak, 'Evening.' A nod received in reply.

I'd been to the restaurant a few times. It had recently undergone renovation, jazzed up somewhat for the Noughties, expanded now to include a takeaway. The waitresses were all Eastern European blondes, the food

46

heart-stopping in both the good and bad way. I'd gone off it when Max was refused entry due to his buggy, which I felt unjustifiable seeing as it was supposedly a family restaurant.

Gladys mentioned that I was categorically *not* to mention the war. When I asked her what Mr F. did like, she said children. I ordered a chicken soup with *Kreplach* and a *Latka*, then rummaged in my bag for a photo of Max.

The situation too forced, with at least a couple of generations between us. To be honest my heart wasn't in it. I wasn't my usual happy-go-lucky self: the past week had taken its toll.

The waitress set down my meal and I tried once again to make contact.

'Mmm . . . just what I need, soul soup.'

No acknowledgement forthcoming.

'Mmm . . . delicious. How's yours?'

He glanced up at me.

'Fine.'

Slowly he turned round to me, shaking his head gently.

'She sent you, didn't she?'

'Who?'

'My wife.'

'Your wife? You married? That's nice. I'm single myself but I have a little boy. Do you want to see a picture of him?'

I know, I know, cringy, but I didn't know what else to say.

'My wife, she sent you, didn't she?' he slowly repeated.

'Well . . . actually,' and I nodded an affirmative. Couldn't pretend otherwise.

'You an escort?'

'Do I look like an escort?'

47

'How would I know?'

'Well, I'm not.'

Conversation ceased. I was affronted by his comments, slurping soup on the defensive, and he sipping a lemon tea reading the *Antiques Gazette*.

I felt the need to explain myself.

'Look, Mr Finklestein, your wife called the company I work for and asked if I'd come down here and talk to you. Just chat. She's worried, says you haven't been yourself these past few weeks.'

'No disrespect, lady, but I'm not interested in talking.'

'Fine, I didn't mean to offend you.'

It wasn't fine. He was curt, bordering on the offensive, and I was thinking did I really look like an escort? On a downward spiral I spun into the negative.

'So you don't want to talk?'

'You have a problem with English?'

'I'm just trying to be friendly.'

'Save yourself the bother. You want to move tables or will I?'

Jesus, but I didn't deserve this, sick to the gills of playing these stupid games. Since the Bob fiasco, my confidence was waning, and here is this old man making me feel small, smaller than him even.

I pushed back the chair and put on my jacket, left enough money to cover the bill, leant towards him and then snapped. I snapped and splurged.

'Mr Finklestein, you are one of the most discourteous men I have ever met.'

'Jeez. Do I have to listen to this? What are you, *meshuggener*?'

No, just a single mum, on the brink of losing it. My mind, my job, my dignity . . . Oh no, my mistake, that went to a total dick a week ago, and unbelievable though it may seem, I also lost a finger. Yep, to top it all I lost a real-life, hacked-off finger.

I stormed out of the restaurant, stood on the pavement taking stock of my life. Christ, and there I'd been feeling sorry for him, just 'cause he was old.

Bastard.

MEN, THEY'RE ALL THE ...

Well, not the same, just disappointing.

My father wasn't very supportive when I'd announced I was going it alone and having Max.

'Every child deserves a father.'

'So what was your excuse?'

'Oh come on, that's totally different. At least you knew who I was.'

'But you weren't there.'

'Issy, you spent every holiday with me.'

They split when I was four and my brother six. It must have been hell for my mother over the next few years. Indeed, I forgave my parents many things when I had a child of my own. Mum didn't have a proper boyfriend till I was ten and I remember being a total bitch to the two of them. No one was allowed time with my mother, yet here's the rub, we allowed Dad his girlfriends. They were somehow more like au pairs and were cool to hang out with. One actually was an au pair.

'Dad, holidays aren't reality, day-to-day living. Fun times are easy, and besides, you always sent Freddie and me off on summer camps.'

'You enjoyed it.'

'Only 'cause I was desperate to spend time around you.'

'There, you proved my point. Max needs a father.'

'You're right,' I conceded. 'Yeah, come to think of it you're going to be a major influence in his life, one of his strongest male role models, so don't go shirking your responsibility.'

Of course Max should have a father but he doesn't, and there's nothing I can do about it, bar providing stable male figures he can relate to. He adores my older brother Freddie, who dotes on Max no end and has begun to take him out shopping. Freddie buys him tight white T-shirts and Prada jeans. He treats Max as a designer accessory, taking him on quick strolls up and down Old Compton Street. I say quick, 'cause the minute Max gets twitchy, I have to go and rescue Freddie. See, Freddie's lifestyle doesn't really cater to small children, though he promises to take him clubbing, when he's in his teens.

OK, so Freddie can't provide the rough and tumble, football, blokesy bond, but they love each other and as far as I'm concerned that's the only thing that matters. And you know, there are times I feel exceptionally lucky being on my own with Max. I've met too many women whose partnerships have broken down unexpectedly after the birth of their child. It really must be quite horrendous to be so suddenly deserted. It comes down to expectations, and as I never had any, it hasn't been an issue.

SINGLE MOTHERHOOD VERSUS THE CONVENTIONAL

I have complete control over how I wish to bring Max up, and he can't play one parent off against the other. There are no compromises to be struck. There is no resentment harboured, such as when one partner has more access to the adult world. This, I believe, is a big bug-bear in many relationships, as my more honest married friends will testify. Max is my sole responsibility and I share him with no one.

The minus being, of course, Max is my sole responsibility and I share him with no one.

THE FICKLE FINGER OF FATE

I guess my luck ran out last week. I put it down to the finger. Since then, near ruin on every front. It was haunting me. Why me? Hadn't I enough on my plate not to be beset upon by flesh and tiny bones?

I trudged home from my meeting with Finklestein to find Maria glue-eyed to *Graham Norton*. She was knitting a jumper for Max. A *Spiderman* one, red background with a big black web on it.

'How'd it go with Finklestein?'

'Not good, he wouldn't speak to me.'

'And?'

'Maria, do I look like an escort to you?'

'What?'

'No, seriously?'

'Listen, Max is a bit cranky, he's coming down with something.'

'Great.'

That's all I needed.

'And a detective called by when you were out.'

'Huh?'

I was hanging up my jacket, yawning loudly.

'He left his number, asked if you'd ring him tomorrow.'

'What did he say?'

'They found the body.'

ONE PLAIN, ONE PURL

Clickity clack went her needles as I made Maria a cup of tea.

'A detective,' she said. 'His name is Bambuss.'

He'd asked if I would be so kind as to call at the first opportunity. A body had been found. A murder? Who's to say? He hadn't elaborated further, no other clues given. He'd had a quick look around the apartment.

'A Cypriot,' remarked Maria. 'Originally from Cyprus, greying at the temples. Very distinguished man – reminded me of that actor, Omar Sharif.'

'Oh.' I perked up, so he had a whiff of the Omar. 'My age?'

'No, my age,' Maria replied.

Maria is the same age as my mother. Olive skin, dark hair, Rubenesque and small, not quite an aged and tubby Penelope Cruz but with a twinkle in her green eyes. Her husband passed away a couple of years back and, instead of crumbling, it's as if she's finally come into herself. Her children have nest-fled to disparate points of the globe and all have children of their own, which means Maria gets to travel quite a bit. She misses being a hands-on gran, though, luckily for me, she's all but formally adopted Max as her grandson.

Her role at the Honey Trap evolved naturally. She'd been cleaning Trisha's house and had done some baby-sitting. Trisha referred her to Fiona, who then took her on.

Time to go. She gathered up her bits and bobs, sighed, and then made the sign of the cross.

'Poor old dear, let's hope she at peace now.'

'Yeah, it's awful. Guess I'll find out the whole story tomorrow. Thanks, Maria.'

Standing in my hallway, I watched as she put on her helmet, bicycle clips and reflector bands, then disappeared on her push bike, off into the night.

BEYOND THE FINGER

I hadn't thought beyond the finger, not really. It hung suspended in my imagination like a novelty. I ignored the fact it had once belonged to a hand, to a living, breathing person. Old women are two a penny, clumping along all over the place with their shopping trolleys. One passes them by, forgetting they were ever young, assuming they were always as they appear: slow-moving, wearing worn-out coats.

My mother, initially a reluctant granny, finally caved in once she saw Max. She spends a month with us every summer. Last time she came, Max and I collected her from the airport. I hadn't seen her for a year and was shocked at how she'd aged. The fine lines had become entrenched, and though she was still very striking, her hair was now grey and she refused to dye it.

Practical by nature, she had given me plenty of advice when I fell pregnant.

'Issy, you want to make sure you have a strong support group around you, find out about as many mother-baby groups as you can and sign up now.'

Unsurprisingly I ignored her advice and came to regret it.

She had a good life in New Mexico: a partner and a job as an office administrator in a production company. She was loath to run to my side and exhaust herself. She'd been there, done it, worn out the T-shirt.

Of course we got on each other's tits no end within twenty-four hours of her arrival, but the summer had been so much sweeter with her around, especially when she gave me a whole seven days and seven nights of freedom in Barcelona.

Mum and I speak about twice a week. When I told her about the finger she, being into the mystical, was convinced it was a sign.

'Your chi is unbalanced. You are dislocated from yourself, Issy – it's time to look within.'

'Mother, I'm totally spent.'

'You need to meditate.'

'Stop with the mumbo jumbo. The fact is I'm straddling two worlds, being single and being a mother.'

'Surrender to your situation. It's the only way forward.'

'How did you cope with the two of us on your own?'

'I got stoned a lot.'

I'd forgotten the sweet herbal smell that was my mother's scent. I know a fair few mothers who puff to relax at the end of a day, some during the day, or who pay a nightly visit to the bottle that takes the edge off the situation and aids a quick exit to sleep.

'Are you advocating I take drugs?'

54

Having spent much of my youth wasted, I'd turned away from the dulled numbness and brain stupefier that is weed.

'I'm just saying, you're trying to do too much and gotta slow down. Your life has changed. There are constraints now, and you have to find a way to work within them.'

She's right and I hate her for it.

I've never subscribed to the idea that motherhood changes one as a person. Fundamentally you remain the same, though perhaps become more patient.

'There's a reason the finger found its way to you.'

'OK, Mum, whatever. So when are you coming over again?'

'The summer. Have you spoken to Freddie lately?'

'Not for a while.'

The last I'd heard from Freddie was a few weeks back, when he went on a major clubbing/drugs binge. I've learnt from previous experiences not to contact him for about a week after, as he is 'coming down', which translates as being a paranoid pain in the arse.

'Mum, do you think I'll ever fall in love again?'

'Give it time, it's bound to happen.'

'But my prime is passing me by. I'm getting ugly, Mother.'

'I'm hearing a lot of negativity, Issy. Are you still going to your group-therapy sessions?'

Oh Christ, that was a laugh.

Nadia had told me how a friend of hers met a really cool man in group therapy. They had since married and were expecting a kid.

'Don't dismiss it – it's a great way to meet people and get a load off your chest.'

So, off I went to my local GP, got an instant referral, easy-peasy. No sooner had the words 'single mother' fled my parted lips than she had me signed up. A week later, I sat in a sterile room surrounded by a bunch of depressives talking about their childhoods and coming to terms with their feelings. I couldn't get a word in and had to listen to some pretty appalling stuff, which incidentally cured me on the spot, as I realised how lucky I was in comparison.

On the male front there were but two, a geezer in his fifties and a younger one. The latter not-too-bad-looking, actually, if I squinted hard, a bit Hugh Grant-ish, if he shaved off his face fur, but alas, he turned out to be married.

Then, like a bolt from the blue, a thwack of a realisation bludgeoned me and I recalled his name ... Bob.

Yeugghhh ... Imagine if it was the same guy. But of course I would have recognised him ... unless that is he had shaved off his beard and tache.

Yeugghhh ...

Nah, surely I would have clicked?

Thrice yeugghhh, as snippets of conversation vomited into my consciousness. Yeah, on recollection, I had been struck by his seemingly genuine sincerity and empathy. Yet, it was inconceivable to marry the email Bob with this one, but now it kinda made sense. The guy was obviously schizoid. Although thinking about it, he was the counsellor.

OWEE OWEE OWEE, MUMMY'S IN BIG TROUBLE

'Max, I've got to see a policeman today,' I announced.

Max lay warm in the bed beside me, all cuddly and edible. One of my main fears when he was a baby was that I'd eat him. I swear, the smell, the soft skin, pink flesh, tiny fingers – I'd bury my face in his belly, gobbling the love off him. Now things have begun to change and his bottom is not quite so endearing, as he blasts the morning chorus, trumpeting the dawn call a little too close for comfort.

'Max! What do you say?' I chastise Mr Fartypants.

'It wasn't me.'

Ah such sweet denials.

'Yes, it was.'

'No, it wasn't. It was you.'

Damn, no longer can I get away with it. He's way too clever for his age and I, guilty, changed the subject.

'I have to meet a detective today.'

'Are you going to prison?'

'Hope not. It's about that finger you found.'

'The finger in the garden?'

'Can I have a kiss?'

'Later, in a few minutes.'

Kisses used to be on tap, whenever I wanted, free access to the Max, but now I ask and have to wait. Unless of course he's tired and unable to fend off my advances.

Oh lovely, beautiful Max and I woke in a good mood, for some unknown reason. Chased Max through the apartment, ending up with a tickling session and much giggling.

DETECTIVE BAMBUSS

Bambuss leant back in his plastic chair, corpulent and hirsute. His chest hair met with his beard line, which was meeting with his forehead. He sat directly opposite me, picking luncheon scraps from between his teeth and then tongue-sucking at the remains. His face wore an air of mild perplexity and he appeared to be looking at me somewhat suspiciously. Omar Sharif? My arse.

'Miss Brodsky, so it was your son who found the deceased's finger?'

'Yes, a week ago, in the garden.'

He asked me questions similar to that of the first policeman.

'And it still hasn't turned up?'

'What, the finger? No, unfortunately not.'

'And, my dear, you've searched everywhere?'

'And some.' I explained the circumstances leading to the loss, then quickly changed the subject. 'So have you found the murderer?'

Intrigued by the gruesome, I wondered if perhaps the culprit was a serial murderer who hacked off his victims' fingers as some kind of trophy.

'Well, my dear, the thing is she wasn't actually murdered.'

'What do you mean?'

'Her finger was hacked off after she died.'

OK, so he was confusing me.

'The finger was hacked off after she died?'

58

Interesting, very interesting, but let's get down to basics: who was the deceased?

THE DECEASED, GOD REST HER SOUL

Sarah Bloch. Originally Viennese, seventy-nine years of age. She lived but two doors down from me in apartment no 24, Antrim Mansions, Antrim Road, Belsize Park. She had been there twenty-five years.

'Tell me, did you know her? Do you recall seeing her out and about?'

'What did she look like?'

'A fine-looking woman, slight in frame, about five foot five. She wore a check tweed coat. Ring any bells?'

'Wait, something's coming.' I focused hard and, through the twitching net curtains of my cerebral matter, a shape, a figure, a . . . 'No, sorry, old women are a dime a dozen.'

'She was very active for her age, worked in a charity shop in St John's Wood.'

Wait . . . I frequent those musty bargain dens. Only a couple of weeks since I tried on an old Agnes B. trouser suit and the woman selling it had said, 'You're getting a bargain,' to which I'd replied, 'That's why I'm here.'

She winced at my feeble wit and muttered something under her breath that I couldn't quite catch.

I asked if they could lower the price even more and she said, 'No.'

I got uppity and replaced the suit on the hanger.

Even though I could have afforded it, even though it looked good on me, even though the colour suited me.

'Your loss,' she'd mumbled as I marched out of the shop, disgusted she wouldn't bargain with me.

I went back the next day, but it had been sold.

'Detective Bambuss, can you be more specific? What exactly did she look like?'

'Still quite beautiful, high cheekbones, slender – you could tell she'd been a looker in her day. Very elegant: she wore her hair scraped back into a high bun.'

No, the lady in the shop was plump with badly dyed hair.

'She'd come out of hospital recently, had fallen down some steps and broken her ankle.'

'So what exactly happened?'

'It appears she was burgled after she died.'

'Burgled, and you don't think she died from the shock?'

'No, it doesn't seem to be the case.'

'I see. And why the hacking off of the finger?'

Aha . . . a picture was forming in my mind.

'I suspect she wore a ring. Hence the finger being hacked off?'

Bingo!

'But why my garden?'

Bambuss smirked, entertained by my mental deductions.

'Perhaps flung from a window?' I mused.

'I'm afraid the distance is too great. We've already ruled that one out.'

'Though of course the gardens are all interconnecting. Perhaps the assailant made a getaway out the back and merely flung the finger by pure chance into my garden. That's possible, highly probable.'

Bambuss smirked, so obviously impressed as I Dr Watsoned to his Holmes.

'And the burglary – tell me more,' I demanded.

'Not a professional job, but whoever did it knew her apartment and what she had.'

'Therefore opportunist. Someone had called to see her, found her dead . . . She knew the culprit, the culprit knew the apartment and where to look.'

By Jove, I think I'm on to something here.

'What about her family?'

'An only son, living in the States.'

'Did she have any friends?'

'A few, the bridge brigade mainly. They met in her house every four weeks.'

'So an acquaintance. You say she'd been in hospital . . . therefore someone would have had access to the apartment. Forgive me, I'm thinking aloud. Yes, it could well be a . . . a neighbour.'

'A neighbour?' echoed the detective.

'Yes, someone who perhaps held a spare set of keys, helped her out occasionally.'

'That's exactly what I was thinking.'

'Great minds and all that,' I declared.

'Tell me, my dear, do you have a liking for jewellery?'

'What girl doesn't.'

Felt an oncoming Ally McBeal moment and suddenly wondered if I was under suspicion. It was the way he was peering at me, whilst nibbling at his nails. Shaggy's song came to mind: 'It Wasn't Me'. Max's all-time favourite, beating 'Bob the Builder' by miles. Imagination hurtled into the surreal as Bambuss crooned accusations and I defended myself, circling about the interview table. *(Picture this, I was caught red-handed murdering the oul' one next door! . . . Did you hack her into pieces? It wasn't me! Chop her up with a bread knife? It wasn't me!)*

REALITY CHECK

The detective stared at me strangely.

'Miss Brodsky?'

'Sorry.'

I snapped back to reality.

'As I was saying, if you recall any suspicious activities, or anything that would be of use in our investigations, please get in touch.'

'Of course.'

'And you don't mind if we have a look around your garden?'

'Not at all. I'm working later, but I'll let Maria know.'

'And your work – what exactly do you do?'

'Well, since you ask, I'm actually a special agent, of sorts.'

MISSION ONE

My maiden voyage into the world of the near adulterous and I, nerve-racked, practised chat-up lines on Max.

'You come here often?'

'I wanna watch a video.'

'Hi.'

'*Thomas* video.'

'Excuse me, is this seat taken?'

'Now!'

Failed abysmally. What chance would I have with an adult male? Nadia's top tips had been to establish eye contact, mirror their body language, and if stuck for something to say, repeat word for word what they had just said, adding an upward inflection.

My first mission. I remember it well.

With knees knocking, I espied my suspect alone at the bar and approached with caution. A free stool beckoned, and I wedged myself up on to it. Just got to be friendly, smile, order a drink and if all else fails, talk about the weather.

Five minutes later.

'It's bitter cold, hey?'

'Huh?'

'It's cold outside.'

'Mmm,' *très*, *très* unresponsive.

Then out of nowhere came a gem of a chat-up line.

'I just split with my boyfriend.'

'Oh.'

The suspect's interest is awakened. Everyone loves a sob story – always makes them feel so much better about themselves.

'I'm sorry, I don't usually come to bars on my own but . . . do you mind if I, well . . . talk with you for a minute?'

So I told him my story, actually told him the truth. Maybe I went on a bit – it was near on an hour later when I finally finished.

'I know how you feel,' he sympathised.

'Do you?'

'Yeah.'

'Are you stuck in a stale marriage?'

'What?'

'I saw your ring.'

'No, I have a healthy marriage, thanks.'

'Guess I jumped to the wrong conclusion. On the rebound . . .'

I blushed, giving him the come-on.

'That's OK, nice talking to you.'

He jumped up and left.

'You too.'

OK, it hadn't exactly gone to plan. I'd expected sleazy, not a kind and generous listener. As far as I was concerned, my suspect was impeccable marriage material. A decent male, so rare a species. But hey, I'm cynical and I downed a quick one for the road and bid the landlord *adieu*, setting off in spirits high and my faith redeemed in mankind.

Tipsy and reporting slurred messages down the mobile to the office, I tripped on the pavement and fell to my knees. My new tights were laddered, and as I rose up from that humbled position, I shifted quickly. Basically to make out I was tying my shoe strap, so as not to be further embarrassed, but also because who should I spot emerging from the opposite doorway? My suspect. I didn't bother to holler after him. For we were in Soho and the sign on the door said 'Live Model'.

CATEGORIES OF DICK

As in any business, we at the Honey Trap have our own classification code.

Clever Dick – See above, the type who uses the services of professionals. They are astute liars and very hard to pin down or expose. We usually caution the wife.

Dick (the honey pot) Dipper – into anything that moves.

Big Dick – a City boy.

Decent Dick – true to his wife.

Premature Dick – a bona fide letch, he loves to lookie,

but no touchie and never nookie. The type mainly found in lap-dancing emporiums.

Dick Dock – wife had forgiven previous adulterous liaison but suspicions have been rearoused.

Slick Dick – gorgeous man, no wonder his wife is insecure.

Private Dick – strictly an Internet adulterer. Chat-room addict, or, as we like to call them, a techno wanker.

WHICH OF COURSE BRINGS US BACK TO BOB

A dickhead. His emails continuing to blast the airwaves. In my heart of hearts, I strongly suspected the finger had fallen out in the car during our entwinement; most likely it slipped down a crack. (No pun intended, so don't even go there.)

I should have come clean and called Bob at work, strictly off the record, and said, 'Look, mate, whatever happened, let's just forget it, and by the way did you happen to find a finger in your car?' Somehow it didn't flow right.

I hate confrontations, always have done. It was three months before I told my boyfriend Finn about Jan. He'd come back from his expedition and the first thing he said was, 'You've put on weight, Issy. Suits you.'

I'd beamed with joy, instead of getting all uppity and angsty, and I guess this made him suspicious. A female happy to expand in girth? Unheard of in Western civilisation.

To be honest, I have never felt more womanly or truly beautiful than when I was pregnant. The fuller the better. My colossal reflection had a luminous glow. I pitied bony women, obsessed with their bodies in their ever more frantic desire to remain young. Everything, bar this new being forming within me, paled into insignificance. How ingenious is the human body was the thought I carried throughout my pregnancy. Says a lot for the hormones, hey? Like totally obliterating one's rationality. Rendering you in effect something not unlike a beached whale going slightly doolally.

Finn was fairly devastated, his trust in me shattered, though I believe he did love me. He couldn't hack it, so he cut off all communication and I haven't seen him since.

After meeting with the detective, I'd moseyed on down to the office to check out my week's schedule. Nadia was in high spirits – she was on a roll, having achieved positive results with her last ten clients. We have a monthly scoreboard, and there's a bonus for the winner. I was lagging way behind, the loser in the race, which I blamed on the tools I'd had the misfortune of having to chat up. Bob, Mr Finklestein . . . I ask you? I mean how could I possibly compete?

I recall saying something similar to my mother, the one year she managed to make it to my school sports day. And I'll never forget the look on her face when I came in last every race. She did her best to smooth over my disappointment, never mind the fact she'd given me a soup ladle for the egg and spoon.

'Nadia, I think someone's put a hex on me.'

She was merrily humming, strumming her fingers on the desk.

'Cool. Hey, Issy, you won't believe it . . .'

I booted the computer to check whether Bob had sent yet another email. There it was, loitering in my inbox with intent: 'Sexy Bob on the horn 4 U. Tell me when, where, I'll be there. xxxxx.

How I wished I was in a position to say, 'In your –'

PIPE DREAMS AND GONADS

'Issy, are you listening? I said it's finally beginning to happen.'

'What?'

'On the singing front.'

'About time.'

'What do you mean?'

'Personally I thought you were past it, you know, like it was a dream you were hopelessly clinging on to.'

In previous moments of creativity, otherwise known as unemployment, I'd started up my own business. Convinced I was on to something big with Pipe Dreams. A revolutionary product, dreams one could hold on to. In effect, salvaged pieces of pipe I'd found in a skip. Neat concept, hey? I tarted them up and put pieces in pretty boxes to sell to twee gift shops. Novelty gifts and I was going to call the company It's the Thought That Counts Ltd. You know how everyone has their own little private fantasies? Well, I reckoned on it being a cutesy, profitable idea. Drew up a proposal for the bank but it met with zero interest, although I did manage to shift a dozen boxes to a shop in Ladbroke Grove.

Nadia took unkindly to my bluntness.

'Thanks for the vote of confidence, Issy.'

'Pleasure.'

'Fuck you.'

'Sorry . . . sorry, I didn't mean it like that . . . So what's the big news?'

'Forget it.'

Nadia was pissed off and I, at least a fortnight away from PMT, had no excuse.

'Nads . . . Nads . . .' I whinnied and whined. 'Aw, Nadia, pleeeeeease?'

'You are such a bitch.'

'Let me guess. You got a record deal?'

'No.'

'A producer heard your tapes and wants to use you.'

'No.'

'OK you won a place on one of the those "Make Me a Star" programmes.'

'No.'

My second fabulous business idea. Sprung forth whilst singing in the kitchen, with Max dancing round my heels. A Robbie number, of course. Had been singing it for the past hour, over and over again, being in one of those femy 'emotional' moods. Oh the longing! Thought it would make a brilliant reality TV programme: *It Could Have Been You!* The premise, not wholly original because it's a *Pop Idol* scenario, but different in being restricted to mothers, i.e. those who have suffered a long line of opportunity knocks. I mean why favour the young? They have a lifetime of false hopes ahead of them. Give the has-beens a chance. One more go at failing fabulously. The tired, strained look of motherhood would lend itself quite well to the occasion. Most of us already have that raccoon-eyed kohl thing going on, albeit natural.

'You won the Lottery?'

'NO.'

'Just tell me your good news.'

She paused for suspense, then spoke very slowly.

'I got a gig.'

'Really?' I came over all green. 'Where?'

'In the pub across the way.'

'Not the –'

'Yeah.'

'When?' I feigning nonchalance.

'In ten days. Isn't it great?'

'Whoopie for you.'

Not fair. So not fair. I wanted something exciting to happen to me. I mean nice exciting, not finding-a-hacked-finger exciting, or fucking-a-Bob exciting. Arms crossed and sulking in my corner.

'Issy, you look exactly like Max when you do that.'

'Do I?' Christ, how far have I regressed?

'So you are going to come and support me?'

'Yeah . . . I mean as long as I can get a babysitter.'

Babysitters being the bane of my life. And expensive – even Freddie charges me. My own sibling and over the going rate, plus I have to make dinner for him. Prior to Maria, I'd used a girl called Kate. An A-level student, nice enough and I thought it would be fine, she could study when Max was asleep, earn a few quid, but she was seventeen.

Seventeen, rubbing my face in the fact that I was older though not wiser. I'm certain since having Max my intelligence has eroded, as one, by default, downgrades to the level of a Tellytubby. I doubt there is a mother out there who, hand on heart, hasn't at one time or another forgotten what day of the week it is.

When I met Kate, I was under the illusion that on a good day I could pass myself off as a yummy mummy. However, beside her, I appeared about as appetising as leftover dog food. To make matters worse she regarded me not as a mate or an equal, but as someone who was past it. I made the mistake of being friendly, and leaving out my Robbie CDs to show her I was still with it. Even went so far as to tell her she could smoke pot if she wanted to. Listen, even I cringe thinking about it now.

The worst of it was, she used to bring her boyfriend with her. Max didn't mind, an extra playmate and all that, but there she was: pretty, pert-titted, flat-stomached and brim full of youthful enthusiasm.

Yes, there she was getting laid on my couch while I'd been out scouring the city for a hint of a basic encounter. My heart goes out to women who have au pairs, especially beautiful ones. Always employ an ugly au pair or you're just asking for trouble.

Barging in on them, mortified, I yelped, 'When you've finished, can you come and see me in the kitchen?'

Half an hour later she came. I could hear her. Jesus, no shame nor embarrassment, then ten minutes on, she and the boyfriend scabbed two cigarettes off me, asked if I'd had a nice time, took the babysitting money and left. I never called Kate after that.

Maria is my sole babysitter at present. The only thing I'm likely to find her astride is her Raleigh Racer, but when she's not sitting for me, she's usually booked up by the other Honeys.

Nadia shot me a look of disgust.

'You have ten days to find a babysitter.'

'OK, OK, I'll do my best.'

And then it occurred to me: Why not marry the gig with the Bob? Loud music meant I wouldn't have to talk to him too much and Maria would be legitimately babysitting. It could work. I consulted with Nadia: she could see no problem. I punched a message into the keyboard and pressed send. Didn't have to wait too long for a reply. Bob must have been online, and luckily he was up for it.

'Hey, Nads, I got a great name for your band.'

'What?

'The Go-Nads.'

Max time upon me. The nursery beckoning, fines levied if not punctual, on the threshold of mummydom, I was halfway out the door.

'The what?' Nadia asked, wide-eyed and bemused.

'The Go-Nads.'

'You're joking?'

'Nah, I can see it: you on stage, lights flashing, the crowd whipped up into a frenzy and chanting, Go, Nad, Go, Nad, Go, Nad.'

THAT'S WEIRD. I WAS JUST THINKING ABOUT YOU

Coincidences, the chances of, and I saw him first. Recognised him from the back, even after near on four years. He was peering at the windows of Habitat on the Finchley Road. I could have walked past and he wouldn't have noticed; instead, his name blared out from my lips.

'Finn!'

Glanced over his left shoulder.

'Issy!'

Max was holding on to my hand, sucking on a lolly. I was really glad he was wearing his cool clothes, that they weren't totally stained and his nose wasn't dripping.

'Issy . . . Wow, is this your son?'

I beamed proudly. OK, so my face exploded with a vast smile.

'Max, this is Finn.'

'Hi, Finn.'

'Issy, he's beautiful.'

'Thanks.'

I always feel slightly weird taking compliments on

71

behalf of Max – he's his own person. My child-rearing philosophy is to treat him at all times as I would wish to be treated myself. That may sound kind of obvious and it should be obvious, but believe me, I've witnessed many parents who regard their offspring as a mini me, or the living bind of their relationship. Or worse, parents who regard their children as lesser people, to be trained and moulded. Never underestimate a child's capacity to understand, think, feel and emote. Granted, they may not initially have sophisticated means of communicating, but I reckon trying to make out what they're saying is part of the joy of being a parent.

'Issy, he's really beautiful. Looks nothing like you.'

The kick-back, the prick of reality. It's always the same. Max by some weird fluke has blue eyes and blond hair. In effect a mini-version of my dream man.

'Finn, you look great.'

He did, like he'd grown into himself. A man, no longer so boyish. The old Finn had shoulder-length, dirty-blond hair and was a skinny student. His hair was now cut short, no signs of receding or baldness. He'd filled out a little and was dressed in the latest street labels, so effortlessly cool.

'So do you,' he replied.

He was lying, of course. As his eyes were still focused on Max, I let it go.

'And Max must be . . . what, three?'

'Three-and-a-half,' Max corrected him.

'Wow . . . and Issy, what are you up to?'

'Being a mum.'

'I mean are you working?'

How come 'Being a mum' never seems to be enough of an answer?

'A little, nothing much. What about you?'

'Things are good.' He reached into his pocket and gave me his card. 'I set up business with a friend. You remember Barney?'

'Barney? What, beautiful Barney who was always taking Es?'

'That's the one.'

'How is he?'

'Married with three kids.'

'Jeez. What about you, any kids?'

'Not yet.'

Semi-uncomfortable pause, so much left unsaid. Do we lift the lid on the past, or wrap things up pronto?

'So what's your company?'

'It's called Craft Design, we're agents for craftspeople.'

There stood my eco-warrior, blew that one, hey . . .

'What, like thatched roofs?'

'Yeah and . . .'

His words were lost on me, the underlying conversation at odds with the spoken one. What I really wanted to ask was is there any love left between us? Was it there in the first place?

Then he laughed and glibly muttered, 'So if you ever need a picket fence.'

Aha, I was grasping at straws, for the picket-fence reference could mean only one thing: a twee little cottage, Mummy at the door, bun in my oven, bread in the oven, Max chasing chickens and Finn off to chop wood in the forest.

'I'll keep you in mind.'

'Good to see you, Issy.'

'You too, Finn.'

He leant forward and pecked me on the cheek, then pushed through the glass doors of Habitat.

'Max, that was an old friend of Mummy's.'

'Did you used to kiss him?'

73

See, even though only three-and-a-half, Max is way clued in.

'Yeah, a long time ago.'

SUPERMARKET SABOTAGE

Five minutes later and Max was sitting in a trolley whilst I pushed it up and down the aisles of Waitrose supermarket.

Picking out a week's worth of groceries and, 'No, Max, let go of the yoghurt now, please.'

Managed to bypass the aisle containing sweets, biscuits and crisps – otherwise known as life in the fat lane – which is more difficult than it sounds, then pulled over at the toilet rolls. I scanned the shelves and dithered indecisively. Couldn't settle on two-ply or three. The latter though more expensive offered two free rolls in a pack of twelve.

My mind was Finn-flooded, rewinding old footage. Ah go on, treat yourself to three-ply, cut down on the chafing. In the background I heard a child whingeing, and by the time I'd reached the meat counter, the little blighter was in a right old fluster. My heart went out to the mother: it happens to the best of us. Cranky kid and one minor blip can set them off. Something as simple as retracting a yoghurt from their mauling paws, 'cause you know they're just going to squeeze it till it bursts open and makes an unholy mess.

By the time we reached the dairy section the kid was screeching wildly, the whole of the supermarket alerted. The child wouldn't let up, and of course it was my kid. I refused to give in, though the Finn fantasies had to go on hold. Max was off on one and I did so want to bark at him, to temporarily lose it.

'What is up with you?'

'I want a yoghurt.'

'You can have one at home.'

His legs kicked out at me and my eyes narrowed to slits. Teeth clenched, I felt like pushing that damn trolley through the glass walls. Max has a fine pair of lungs, and people had started giving him those 'I feel so sorry for you' looks.

And then one of the bakery assistants arrived over with a gingerbread man to placate the child, my child, and hey presto –

Max fell silent.

Within an instant, he transformed back to sweetness and light. How I wish my emotions could work so fast, so well, that I could go from white rage to placid blue in nanoseconds flat. It's wearying, draining. You can't lose it, not totally, and fuck it: where was my gingerbread man? I wanted something sweet and calming – bottle of Rioja would have to do.

We joined the slowest-moving queue in the world. Wound up, I bit my nails in frustration then despair when Max decided he wanted more. Really wasn't sure I could survive another screaming tantrum without joining in. Damn that interfering assistant. Bribery is lazy parenting, treats should be exactly what the word is, a treat. Now Max would expect a gingerbread man on every shopping trip; he was already beginning to holler again. The upshot being, I lost my place in the queue and went to get him another.

Max never has tantrums. I swear it was unusual behaviour. That said, parents have a habit of lying, especially regarding sleeping patterns. How many times have I heard, 'Oh little Damian sleeps through and has done since the day he was born.' Yeah right, so how come you look so haggard and aged, not to mention that twitch in your left eye.

It wasn't until we'd got back to the apartment that I discovered the reason for his outburst. Bath times can be so revealing and there it was . . .

A POX

All stations on high alert. One pox spied on belly, left of button. Half an hour later, two more appeared. Crankyface came over all cuddlesome and 'I want my mummy'. I obliged, felt guilty for having been so short with him. Had not the nursery posted a sign up of late, informing parents there was a case of the chicken pox! How could I have been so stupid, so very . . . human. That was it then: I knew for the next week Max and I would be incommunicado.

HOLED UP

In Horrorville. Max was not a pretty sight. A quick visit to the GP confirmed my suspicions. We were advised to lie low.

'Keep him in for a week or so and stay clear of pregnant women.'

Too late, the waiting room had been full of them. All first-timers, and they'd been cooing at Max, having that first-timer's romanticised view of children. There are occasions when the sight of a pregnant woman fills me with dread and I want to cry out, 'Wipe that inane smile off your face. Have you any idea what is entailed?'

Let's face it, parenting is a minefield.

A QUICK TEST TO SEE IF YOU'D BE A GOOD PARENT

1. Are you a patient, giving, loving, nurturing, selfless person who is unaffected by loss of sleep and always in control of your emotions?

    If you have answered yes, you are obviously totally delusional and will be a crap parent.

2. Are you neurotic, wired, selfish, emotionally needy and prone to thoughts of is this really my life?

    If you have answered yes, you already are a parent.

3. Are you basically a good human being, emotionally balanced, financially balanced and willing to sacrifice yourself for another?

Yes?

Really?

OK, so then the chances are you may well be a good parent. You'll do your best, you'll do your duty, by God and by country, and for what?

For your darling progeny to reject you anyway.

Ha!

As decreed by the laws of teenagity, it is understood that upon reaching double digits, perhaps even earlier, your child will begin to reject you, and it is highly likely you will be taunted with such standard lines as: 'I hate you,' 'I didn't ask to be born,' etc.

I called the office.

Trisha, obviously stressed, spat down the phone, 'Well, that's just bloody typical of you, Issy. Your timing is impeccable. Last night the phones were hopping, we're short-staffed as it is, Fiona has just been given the date of her operation, and now you've let us down.'

'Trisha, it's not my fault.' Hey, and spot the scapegoat. I did my utmost to appease her. 'Look, I can still work if Maria can sit.'

Damn, but I badly needed to bolster my numbers or I'd be the monthly loser three times in a row.

She didn't sound convinced, and said she'd call back.

The nursery informed me of their scab policy. Max would not be let in again until each and every scab had healed, which meant two weeks as opposed to one.

'Ms Brodsky, I understand your situation but it's too risky. Basically if the scab falls off in nursery, the other children could pick it up and . . . eat it.'

Realistically, I was looking at ten days of full-time motherhood with no respite. Thankfully I'd a fully stocked fridge, but what about entertainment? Solved easily enough – a quick jaunt down to the local video shop with a well-wrapped-up Max.

Trisha called back, having spoken to Maria, whose pregnant daughter just happened to be over for the week. There was no way she'd sit for me. Stressed to the nth, Trisha barked down the phone at me, while Max hollered. Piggy in the middle, I was getting a tirade of abuse in each ear, Trisha down one and Max down the other.

'Trisha I'm going to have to go.'

'Mummeeeee, Mummeeee,' in that high-pitched whine that hurts the eardrum.

'Oh and another thing – some old dear called, a Mrs Finkletin.'

'You mean Finklestein.'

'Said she wants you to ring her – something about her husband.'

'Mummeee, Mummeeeeeeeeeeeeeee.'

'In a minute, Max. What's the number?'

'Mummeeeeeeee.'

'Trisha, just text me the number, Max is going ape.'

Poor fella, uncomfortable in his own skin. My own head about to explode, my brain near spasming. I was going to lose it for sure and then time stood still, seconds turned to hours, minutes to days, hours to weeks. Everything seemed to fuse and I couldn't remember much after that.

DAY TWO

Interminable boredom averted by a rat-a-tat-tat. I opened the door ever so slightly and peeked out at my visitor. 'Twas only the Detective Bambuss.

'Hello, my dear, is this a good time to have a look in the garden?'

'As long as you're not pregnant.'

'Do I look pregnant?'

Well, the hard rotund belly perched above and over-flowing his trouser belt did, it must be said, resemble that of a nine-monther.

'Max has the chicken pox.'

I slide the chain from across the door.

'Don't worry, I've had it. Miss Brodsky, let me introduce Stephan Bloch.'

And there I was dressed only in me T-shirt and socks. Lord above, but the state of me, and of the place, and of the child running naked, clothed only in lashings of calamine.

'Who is it, Mum? Who are you?' Max demanded of the well-shod, terribly handsome gent, say mid to late forties and not wearing a wedding ring.

'Hey, little man, what's up? Hear you got chicken pox,' said in that irresistible, gentle American accent and he phenomenally child-friendly to boot.

I opened the door wider, till the hinges creaked.

'No problem, come in, come in. Sorry about the state of the place, and oh –'

'Don't worry, this isn't a social visit.'

It was to me, mate.

The detective strode into the hall and Stephan after him.

I, overcome by social embarrassment, tugged at the ends of my T-shirt and showed the pair of them down to the kitchen and through the back door to the garden.

'Sorry to hear about your mother,' I blurted. 'Very unusual circumstances.'

'Thanks,' he replied. 'Thanks.'

'I'll leave you to it, Detective. Best get dressed.'

It was afternoon. Christ, what must they have thought, slobbo mum with wild child, but they were immersed in more important business. I dragged Max into my room and dressed us both in record time. A mere fifteen minutes later, the door to my bedroom opened and out we trotted.

The detective and swoonable male were, unfortunately, on their way out.

'Thanks for that, Miss Brodsky.'

Quick, think – stalling tactics.

'Won't you stay for a cup of tea or coffee?'

'No but thank you, my dear.'

Bambuss glanced down at his watch.

I managed to get to the door before them, blocking them with conversation.

'So how's the investigation going?'

'Fine, fine. We are making headway.'

'Anyone I know?'

The detective gave me a quizzical stare.

'Confidential information.'

'I won't tell anyone. You can trust me.'

'No formal arrest made as of yet, but we have our suspects.'

The detective stretched out his arms, fingers entwined, and cracked his knuckles. He gave off a strong smell of garlic and stale alcohol. I took a step back.

'Ah go on, give us a clue.'

'My dear . . . you'll be the first to know.'

Hoped he wasn't insinuating it was me.

'And Mr Bloch, are you staying in your mother's apartment?'

'For a while. Gotta wrap up her estate.'

Hmm . . . so he'd be around for a bit.

'I see, yes, well . . . please call by any time.'

Flutter, flutter went my lashes.

'Can you open the door?'

'Oh silly me.'

Cringe, cringe went my conscience.

Max had taken all his clothes off again and sped by on his scooter.

'Cute kid,' said the delectable Stephan.

'Thanks,' I simpered.

The detective coughed and then muttered, 'Doesn't look anything like you.'

'Yes . . . well . . . Detective, if I can be of any further assistance, you know where I am. Oh and Mr Bloch, I'm really, really sorry I lost your mother's finger. Can't believe I was such a klutz.'

I donned my 'I'm so silly' expression.

'Yeah, I thought that was weird.'

Had to end the conversation on an up note, and the following flew out of my lips, 'I'm sure it'll turn up. Fingers crossed . . .'

Jesus, I can't believe I actually said that.

For the rest of the day, I fixated on Stephan. See, some good had come of finding the finger – it had led to us meeting one another. For the first time in an age, I had glimpsed a man I actually found incredibly attractive. He was so very handsome, so very tempting, so very available. So to cut a long story short, I put him to good use when I went a bush wandering later that night.

ITCHY AND SCRATCHY

On the things one can do with a bog-roll tube, a piece of card, some crayons, Sellotape, glue and scissors, if, and here's the proviso, one is artistic. Unfortunately the rocket ship failed to orbit, the paper boat sank, the Fat Controller remained a bog roll and hard-boiled egghead. Max and I stretched our imaginations to cracking point. The kitchen table transformed into a plane, with two chairs in front as the cockpit. A large cardboard box became a boat, the sofa cushions were pieces of bread, we took turns lying down between them and making human sandwiches. Scattered cushions throughout the flat were used as stepping stones, as we did our best to avoid the snappy crocodile. We also indulged in some monster-baiting, as the place was metaphorically infested. I made special monster nets out of the front-room ones. Besides, I needed new ones anyway.

Disappointed with his catch or lack of, Max asked, 'Where are the real monsters, Mum?'

'Everywhere, Max. They hide themselves in other people.'

'No way.'

'Yeah way.'

'And what do they look like?'

'Normal . . . you got be alert twenty-four seven. Swear to you, kid, it's a dog-eat-dog world out there.'

Thus ended Max's first lesson in paranoia.

Yes, I admit, it was a cruel thing to say but I was slowing losing it. Crawling the walls in Spiderman fashion. Then later on, that very night . . .

NEE NAW NEE NAW

It was bound to happen. The men in white coats appeared, perhaps in answer to my celestial call. I, nose pressed to the net-less window, had been alerted by the sonorous wailing of the ambulance pulled up right outside my gaff. I was half tempted to: a. run to my room and pack an overnight bag, b. shout out, 'What took you so long?' and c. get down on my knees and give thanks for small mercies. The fact was I'd just drunk half a bottle of red. Instead I remained, transfixed, in a near panic-induced state of catatonia, watching the amubulance crew alight from the vehicle. Then I heard someone from upstairs run down and open the front door.

Shit. They'd got here before me. I let out a wistful, 'Nooooooooooooo!'

How could it be? I ran out into the hall and there was Mrs O'Whatshername, a middle-aged Irish woman. Having lived in the block five years I still, shame on me, didn't know any of my neighbours' names. The crew were disappearing up the stairs with a stretcher in tow.

'What's happened?'

'Ah, it's dreadful, awful . . . The man above you, found him out cold, lying on the floor of his flat.'

'Oh my God . . .' I gasped.

So that was the reason for that loud crash nearly an hour ago. The one that had elicited the following response from my good self: banging the ceiling with the top of the broom and throwing curses upwards. My upstairs neighbour, whom I'd last encountered clasping his head in agony and upon whom I had wished a brain haemorrhage, was now 'out cold'.

Oops.

Guess my curse fell back down upon me, and I felt damned.

Mrs O'Whatshername, in shock, launched into the whys and wherefores.

'There was I, watching the telly, next thing, heard this God-awful bang and all the lights went out.'

'And then what?'

'I keep a torch handy at all times . . . sure, the wiring in this building is yonks old. I went to the fuse box, flicked on the switches. But I noticed his lights hadn't come on, which I thought odd. Sure, I knew he was in, had said hello to me earlier in the evening . . .'

Cut to the chase, cut to the chase, woman.

'Here now, I said to myself, there's surely something amiss. So I went knocking on his door, nothing happening, no reply, called out his name, nothing, and you know what, I thought ah he's just gone out, but then . . .'

What? What . . . ?

'Now, I'm not one to snoop, but something was telling me to shine the torch in through his letter-box. So I did, and God love him . . . didn't I just see his feet and him laid out on the ground like a corpse.'

'Like a corpse, you say?'

'A dead man.'

The crew were making their way back down the stairs. My neighbour lay prone, belted on to the stretcher. Eyes closed, an oxygen tank at his side.

By this stage, I was near gagging on guilt. I'd killed him.

Mrs O'Whatshername turned her attention from me and went to talk to one of the crew. I stood at the entrance, watching as they loaded my neighbour into the back of the ambulance.

Mrs O' stood a few feet away.

'I see, I see . . . Oh that's terrible . . . Oh please God . . . All right, I will do . . . Thank you . . . And God bless yous.'

The ambulance drove off at high speed. Mrs O' and I stepped back into the communal hallway. She closed the door, a clenched fist pressed against her mouth, pulling her cardy close about her body.

'How is he?'

'Unconscious.'

'God, that's awful. Will he live?'

'Up a ladder, changing a bulb, then – wham. Jesus, but you never know what's round the corner.'

She sighed heavily and slow-marched back up the stairs.

My fault, all my fault . . . Back in the flat, I sank

the rest of the red wine. Then did that praying thing again.

DEAR GOD,

Seems I may have inadvertently wished death on my neighbour, who is currently fighting for his life. I swear, it wasn't on purpose, well, at the time it was, but I've since seen the error of my ways. So I was wondering if you'd be open to doing a deal. Let's say, I don't mind losing my job or maybe just letting that whole stinking Bob mess unfurl, but please, please, can you just see that the guy doesn't die? I don't think I could bear it. Thanks for that.
Your faithful friend,
Issy.
PS I will try from now on to be an even better person.

SIBLING REVELRY

The intervening days lagged. It wasn't so much Max, as we spent most of our time playing. Rather it was the lack of adult interaction. Freddie turned up eager to offload his relationship problems, or lack of. I, on the other hand, was miffed he hadn't called round sooner, considering the number of messages I'd left.

He was looking kinda peaky – his skin had gone a weird tone.

'Are you taking too many drugs?'

'Issy, you're beginning to sound like a mum.'

'I am one. Freddie, you're turning a shade of orange.'

'What are you talking about?'

It was true. Max, Freddie and I compared flesh tones.

'See, you're orange-tinted. What are you on?'

Freddie, a bona fide gym freak, was on a mission to become a Muscle Mary and in the name of Adonis pumped heaploads of chemical shit into his body.

I handed him his dinner, a plate of tinned tuna, he being on a protein-only diet, and I mused, 'No wonder you're not with anyone, you look diseased,' which in retrospect was not the kindest thing to say, as appearance was everything to Freddie.

He shot off a string of nasty comments, stinging missiles of hurt, like only a sibling can.

I returned the favour and for the next half-hour we argued in silence, or until Max piped up with, 'Look, Mum, Freddie's crying. Give him a kiss.'

So . . . he apologised, I apologised and even Max apologised.

Freddie then came clean, admitted he was sick to the gills of casual encounters. Frustrated, he yearned for a proper relationship, dreamed of finding Mr Right, hankered for that time when everything would click into place and it would be easy, no more searching.

'There is a guy who meets all the requirements.'

'But?'

'I'm not a hundred per cent into him. Sure, he's nice. I like him loads and he's big into me.'

'A bit too much information there,' my mind having conjured up disturbing images.

'Anyway, he wants to have a serious relationship and I want to have a serious relationship.'

'But, not with him?'

'Maybe if we tried we could be happy.'

'For what it's worth, Freddie, that's kinda a pipe dream.'

'No wonder your business venture failed. It's so obvious you never believed in your own product.'

'It won't work if your heart's not in it. Take the Honey Trap, for example. May as well be a lonely hearts club, wives bent by insecurity, disenfranchised husbands staying out 'cause anything is better than going home. Fuck it, these people are lonely as hell and what's worse, they thought they had it all wrapped up when they signed the contract.'

'You are so cynical.'

'No. I'm a realist.'

'OK, Issy, so you're telling me if some guy came along willing to take you and Max on, and he wasn't like your number one choice but fulfilled most requirements . . . you're telling me you wouldn't jump at the chance?'

'Not if I didn't love him.'

'Bullshit.'

'Hey, I'd love to fall in love but I don't need to compromise. I've done it on my own without the trimmings. Life isn't perfect but Max and I are doing fine.'

'So what are you saying?'

'Keep looking.'

'I'm tired of being on my own.'

'Snap, but it'll happen, believe me.'

Hark at Ms Independent: theoretically I believed my own rhetoric. In practice though, chance would be a fine thing. Hadn't seen the handsome American and was losing faith in the prognosis that the finger had brought us together. Though I did manage to bump into Mrs O'Whatshername, mainly to find out her name and also for an update on my near-dead neighbour.

We collided in the hallway as she was on her way out.

'Ah, he's doing nicely. Will be as right as rain in no time, though he took a bad knocking. Should be home soon enough. I'll tell him you were asking for him.'

'Oh . . . OK.'

'Eh and I hope you won't think this awful rude of me, but what's your name?'

See, it takes two to tango.

So, we introduced ourselves and invites to drop by were exchanged.

'Sure you know, I often watch you and your son playing out in the garden. He's a credit to you. Such a happy little chap.'

So said Mrs Lynch before tootling off to the hospital with a bag of grapes.

I watched her go, thinking I should make more of an effort with the neighbours: they really weren't so bad after all.

BOB'S YOUR UNCLE

Maria arrived up at mine sporting a new bike helmet. 'Twas the night of the gig. Nadia had been sweating adrenalin all day and appeared sleeker than usual when I arrived at the pub.

'Nads, you look like a star.'

She beamed, sparkled, decked out in a silver boob tube and silver hot pants. I, too, had made an effort on the dress front, with a plunging neckline and push-up bra. After all, tonight I was to be Trixi.

Trisha had kindly reminded me of this and of the fact that I had never returned Mrs Finklestein's call. Clear blue forgot all about it.

'Can you do it soon – she's withholding payment till you do.'

Furthermore, Trisha had emailed Bob reminding him of the date, to which he'd replied he couldn't wait. I, on the other hand, could. I'd spent the day rehearsing tactics. How the hell was I going to handle this? Badly, probably. My first foray back into the adult world since Max's pox and the last thing I wanted to be doing was revisiting a one-night stand.

I arrived at eight, on time, and positioned myself by the bar, i.e. highly visible. At nine, Silver Rider (don't ask me why, Gonads is a way better name) took to the stage and began their set. Nadia sounded a bit like a cross between Stina Nordenstam and P. J. Harvey. Meaning, she sounded amazing. I mean she could make it big. My mate Nadia, my best buddy, my loyal friend, heck, we may as well be sisters, had the potential to be a huge star. I was blown away.

I was also blown out.

Bob never showed up. On my tod all evening and ne'er a sight of the dick.

A group of teenage guys, sat in the corner, kept pointing over to me and sniggering.

Then one of them, a ginger-haired ug bug, had the friggin' nerve to come up and say, 'See my mate over there, well, he fancies the pants off you –'

'And?'

'He wants to know if you'll cop off with him.'

'Get lost.'

When the set finished I attempted to join Nadia backstage, but her whole family had flocked to her side. I felt left out, the outsider, and my mood sank.

It irked to be stood up by Bob. It wasn't like I should care, but I did. Plus seeing Nadia up on stage strutting her stuff and surrounded by so much love served only to compound my own sense of stagnation.

Ego battering

Create a dark, blue stinking mood with this quick and easy method. Success assured.

You'll need:

One fragile ego

One address book containing old beaux' numbers

One phone

One soulful CD (optional)

And a box of tissues.

Method

Flick through your address book and choose a number (works best if you are of a slightly nervous and apprehensive disposition). Dial the number and well . . . here's one we made earlier.

'Hi, Finn, it's Issy.'

'Hi, Issy.'

'Came across your number, thought I'd give you a call.'

'Sure – how's that cute boy of yours?'

'Great, just over the chicken pox.'

'I'm sorry, didn't know he was sick.'

'Well, he's fine. So what are you up to?'

'I'm busy at the moment. Can I, er – call you back?'

'I won't keep you.'

'What's up?'

'Actually, I was . . . I was . . . wondering if you'd like to come for a drink sometime?'

'Eh . . . guess I should have told you before . . . I'm getting married next month.'

'Oh . . . oh . . . Congratulations.'

'Thanks.'

'. . . . . .'

'Issy, you OK?'

My voice rose an octave and I blurted out the following:

'Yes . . . see you then. Bye.'

Let the receiver slip out of your palm, and in a state of self-pity and shock, turn on your CD player as loud as possible and then let those tears downward flow.

BATHE ME IN BEAUTY

The following morn on the way back from the nursery, I happened upon a certain American gent, which lifted my sunken spirits.

Fuck Finn, he was yesterday's news.

Stephan was on his way into the block and I hollered out a friendly, 'Hiya.'

He looked at me blankly.

'I'm Issy. You and the detective called by the apartment about a week ago.'

So much for lasting first impressions then.

'Issy with the little boy.'

He put down several bags of shopping.

'Sorry, I didn't recognise you dressed.'

'Ha, ha, ha,' I did flirtatiously giggle.

'How's your son?'

'Better, thanks, and how's everything with your mother – the investigation?'

'Detective Bambuss appears to have everything under control.'

He paused and then suggested coffee.

It was only 10 a.m. – a tad early for 'coffee', hey?

'So you wanna grab a quick coffee?'

'Oh, a coffee . . . yeah, sure.'

I love snooping in other people's homes, taking a peek at how they live. Sarah Bloch had occupied the first-floor flat: the layout was similar to my own. There was a grand piano in the drawing room and the walls were covered with photos and pictures.

Stephan disappeared into the kitchen, leaving me to scan the many images of this woman whose finger I'd found. It felt eerie, unsettling, to come face to face with her. Indeed she had been beautiful and from what I could make out a concert pianist. In amongst various other photos, I spotted ones of Stephan as a child, with an elderly couple. I presumed they were his grandparents.

'Your mother must have been an incredible woman.'

'She was a fine player. There's some recordings of hers, if you want to listen,' he hollered from the kitchen.

'Yeah, I'd love that.'

He reappeared carrying a tray with a pot of coffee, mugs and some biscuits.

'So did you grow up here, in London?' I asked.

'No, I grew up with my grandparents. Sarah used to travel a lot with the orchestra.'

'And what about your dad?'

'Sarah broke up with my father before I was born.'

'A single mum?'

'Guess so.'

'Just like me.'

Isn't there a saying or home truth that most men marry their mothers? Potentially, I was in with a chance and began flicking my hair accordingly.

We skimmed over the usual topics. I discovered

Stephan was a divorced father of two, a lawyer specialising in film who lived in Palo Alto, California. He told me he'd had a strained relationship with his mother, although in the past few years they had begun to get close.

She, I learnt, had grown up in Vienna. Before the war broke out, she'd won a music scholarship to an American college, which basically saved her and her family's lives. Successful, she played professionally most of her life, until her fingers, racked with arthritis, forced her to give it up a couple of years back. In her early forties, she settled in Europe, having married a conductor. He passed away ten years ago.

'So what's your story?' asked Stephan.

Not wishing to outstay my welcome, I suggested we leave it for another day. Clever ploy, hey?

'Damn, is that the time? I really should get going.'

'Sorry, I didn't mean to keep you.'

'No, it's fine, but call me if you're not too busy. It would be nice to hang out.'

We exchanged numbers.

I skipped home, heart all aflutter, and congratulated myself on playing it fairly cool this time.

STANDING UP TALL, TO FALL ALL THE HARDER.

Nadia dropped by to ask for a favour, hyper with excitement. Her whole life was on one big upward turn. There at the gig, unbeknownst to her, was an A & R man lurking in the shadows. He had listened well and then called her, wanting to set up a meeting.

Down on her knees, she begged, 'Issy, please, please, will you do my shift tonight?'

'Sure, no problem,' but on the condition that, when she became very famous, she would invite me to all the swell parties.

'Course I will.'

'Can I have it in writing?'

'Don't you trust me?'

'It's just, fame has a way of changing people.'

'What are you like?'

A hairball of pent-up frustrations, though beginning to unwind on sweet thoughts of the American.

'I may have met a man, Nadia.'

'Really?'

'The son of the finger woman.'

'Is he cute?'

'Dreamy. He's intelligent, good-looking . . .'

And just when I was about to launch into a poetic spiel worthy of my newfound crush, Nadia interrupted the flow with, 'Omigod, I forgot to tell you.'

'What?'

'You know Trisha has been acting kinda odd lately?'

'Like yeah . . . though I thought she just had it in for me.'

'Listen to this.'

Nadia, on her way into the office, had come to a halt outside the door on hearing raised voices from within. The voices belonging to Fiona and Trisha.

The latter shouting, 'I can't take this any more, it's over.'

The former replying, in words to the effect, 'One more chance, please, just one more chance?'

'Fiona, I've tried, I . . .'

'Please, Trisha, don't go . . . we can talk about it.'

'I'm sick of talking.'

The door had swung open, revealing an embarrassed Nadia.

'Oh for fuck's sake. How long have you been outside?'

Before Nadia could even reply, Trisha had stormed off in the foulest of tempers.

'Fiona was snivelling into a hanky. I didn't know what to do.'

'Christ, do you think those two are together?'

'It looked like it.'

We both imagined the scenario, then in unison squealed like a pair of school-girls, 'Gross.'

Trisha and Fiona – who'd have thought? I'd always suspected Trisha was a lesbian but Fiona was an in-betweener.

'I wonder how long it's been going on.'

'It could be ages.'

'Fiona could even be the father of Trisha's children.'

'Do you think?'

'Possible.'

'Scary.'

I know some women get a kick out of emasculating their men, but to have him change sex? The lengths people go in the name of love – it never ceases to amaze. Take Mrs Dodd, for example.

TOO GOOD TO BE TRUE

Once upon a time, though not so long ago, a woman called Betty decided to test the love of her husband. At the age of twenty-one, Betty had married her childhood sweetheart, a lorry driver called Ron, who was faithful to her in every way. Rarely did they fight and, if they did, they made up almost immediately. He was kind, considerate, respectful, a loving husband and good father to their three children.

Together they led a charmed life. Betty had little to worry about. However, when her youngest started primary school, Betty found herself with time on her hands. Too keep herself busy, she took up gardening.

One day, when she was tending her herbaceous border, her neighbour, a bitter, twisted woman called Vera, popped her head over the garden fence and upon exchanging a few words, offered Betty a packet of fast-growing seeds called Doubtus Insecuritus. In truth, she poisoned Betty's simple mind with ill thoughts of falsehoods and deceit.

'A lorry driver! Well, you're a brave woman,' sneered Vera.

'How so?' replied the naive Betty.

'Away from home every other night – who knows where he may be parking his lorry.'

Vera qualified her statement with outlandish tales of dastardly philandering truck drivers and loose women.

To make matters worse Vera called by the next morning with disturbing news. A curvaceous and licentious woman had moved into the house three doors down from her. A woman with red hair and four children born of four different fathers.

'You'd want to watch her,' warned Vera. 'Reeks of trouble.'

Not three weeks had passed when Betty, on her way home from the butcher's, noticed her husband's lorry parked outside their house.

'Strange he should be home so early,' she pondered, but she was happy nonetheless and imagined how they could spend the afternoon together.

However, her joy was shortlived when she caught

sight of him strolling out of their new neighbour's house, carrying his tool box.

'What, in the name of God, have you been up to?' Betty demanded.

'Just helping out our new neighbour,' explained Ron matter-of-factly.

'Doing what exactly?' demanded Betty.

'The woman had a flood on her hands, of biblical proportions. She was in a right old state.'

'So you sorted her out, did you?'

'Course I did, Betty.'

'Being neighbourly, were you?'

'Course I was, Betty.'

Poor Betty – for the seeds sown had taken hold, and were destroying all the good in her. Racked by such destructive feelings and encouraged by her confidante Vera, she arranged through the Honey Trap to test her husband's faithfulness. Vera suggested to her husband Phil that he ask Ron out for a few bevvies with the boys and a trip to the dogs.

To the dogs indeed.

Ron, having no interest whatsoever in greyhound racing, reluctantly agreed to go.

Vera and Betty would follow on incognito.

HELL HATH NO FURY

She was a woman scorned and I her target.

Poor Ron, I'd cornered him, claiming I was a niece of an old friend of Phil's. It was a set-up – what more can I say? Out of politeness Ron did listen to me prattle on till Betty, flushed with rage, came screaming through the crowd, swearing and spitting, pushing Ron this way and that, and then smacked me in the face with a closed fist.

WHOA, BLACK BETTY, NAH NAH NAH.

'I'm going to kill her,' I blubbered.

Maria was wrapping ice cubes in a tea towel, ready to apply to my left eye, which was now all the colours of the rainbow.

I'd stood in complete shock as Betty's hand, in slow motion, inched its way directly towards my face, her fat pudgy fingers adorned with rings. Her mouth open wide, swear words cascading forth. Vera, at her side, arms folded defiantly, egging her on.

Ron, saintly soul that he was, had gasped, 'No, Betty, don't!' and he having just told me what a wonderful woman his wife was.

Came to a total standstill, as if I'd fled my own skin and spirit scarpered. Next thing I knew, I'd been bundled into a cab and was on my way home.

'He was meant to be Nadia's dick,' I wailed.

'You'll be fine,' Maria cooed, doing her best to calm me down.

The shock was subsiding and the realisation rising of how very vulnerable I was. If anything should happen to me, who would look after Max? Thoughts from the back of my mind rushed forth. I should write a will, insure myself against a worst-case scenario.

'Maria, I don't get it – everything is going wrong.'

'You'll be fine, stop worrying. It's not as bad as it looks.'

What the hell was that supposed to mean?

It really couldn't look any worse.

Maria dabbed my eye and I noticed something different about her.

'Maria, are you wearing lipstick?'

'It's quite nice, no?'

FREAK ON FREAK

Two freaks on a windy morning.

FREAK ONE: What the hell happened?

FREAK TWO: What does it look like? (*Pause, then deadpan*) I got into a fight.

FREAK ONE: Did you win?

FREAK TWO: No.

FREAK ONE: Better luck next time.

FREAK TWO: Thanks. How did your brain-haemorrhage operation go?

FREAK ONE: What brain-haemorrhage operation?

FREAK TWO: The one you were in hospital for. (*God bless, but he must have lost a portion of his cranial matter.*)

FREAK ONE: You thought I had a –

FREAK TWO: Yeah, all those migraines you were having.

FREAK ONE: No, I fell, knocked myself out. I was changing a bulb, got an electric shock, lost my footing on the ladder and was flung six feet downwards. I cracked my skull.

FREAK TWO: That's a relief, I thought you'd nearly died.

FREAK ONE: I did nearly die.

(FREAK ONE rubs his bandaged head while FREAK TWO deftly touches her swollen bruised shiner of a black eye. FREAK TWO pushes her key into her door latch.)

FREAK TWO: Well . . . take care.

FREAK ONE: Yeah . . . you too.

MY PROTECTOR

'What happened, Mummy?' Max asked, prodding the swollen skin. 'You look horrible.'

'It was an accident. I was in the wrong place at the wrong time.'

'Who did it, Mum? Tell me, I won't be angry.'

This is exactly what I said when he came back from nursery with a scratched face and pinch-sized bruises on his arm.

'A woman hit me by mistake.'

'Not nice,' he said, and then asked in the sweetest tone of voice, 'Do you want me to kill her?'

My little protector, hunter, always running ahead of me and into everything, his curiosity knowing no bounds. From the moment Max could walk, he was picking up sticks to wave at passing prey, though in the main he'd chase birds and squirrels.

THE WAY I SEE IT

Through one eye, and feeling like a battered wife, having received more attention from passing strangers than in God knows how long, I made my feelings clear to Trisha.

'We should sue the bitch.'

Trisha scratched her chin.

'I wish it was that easy. I received a fax from Betty's solicitor today, saying they were going to sue us.'

I was incredulous.

'What? The woman attacked me. Is she totally crazy?'

'Apparently, there's some archaic trade law that we may be in contempt of.'

'What!'

Trisha began reading the faxed statement.

'"My client's husband was unfairly tempted, as the woman in question was considered too attractive, the likelihood being that most heterosexual males would find it difficult to fend off such advances."'

'That's absurd. It's total bullshit as well.'

'I know.'

(I let Trisha's underhand insult go.)

'But if it goes to court, we could be threatened with closure.'

'What about our satisfied clients?'

'They're all going through costly divorces, and don't want to get involved.'

'So I'm not going to be compensated.'

'Issy, did you hear what I said? We could have to close.'

'You can't friggin' well blame me for this.'

'I wasn't going to.'

'Makes a nice change.'

Trisha and I were caught in a moment of stalemate.

'Issy, as you won't be able to work till your eye heals, Fiona and I have decided you can make up the hours running the office. This place needs a thorough spring clean.'

'And there I was, thinking I'd be granted sick leave.'

'Hazard of the job, I'm afraid.'

'Does it say that in the fine print?' This woman was pushing me to the limit. 'Know what, Trisha, maybe I should call a solicitor.'

'Is that a threat?'

'What the fuck is your problem?'

'And another thing, have you called Mrs Finklestein yet?'

Pronounced pincer digit movements and Gladys's

voice on speaker phone, for the benefit of *mein Führer*, Trisha.

'Hello, you've reached the Finklesteins. Sorry, but we're unable to answer your call. For the next couple of months we're in Florida . . .' Her voice abruptly changed tone as she groaned, 'What, Joel?' the message interrupted by background grumbling, then, 'What date?' More grumbling then, 'You think you should do it? You do it . . . if you're so . . .' Beeeeeeeeep.

God damn it and heavens to Murgatroyd, I left the following message:

'Hi, Gladys. It's Issy here from the Honey Trap returning your call. Please can you call me when you get this message. Thanks.'

A cold-war silence descended between Trisha and me, lasting an hour until Nadia flounced into the office, whereupon she gave me some much-needed attention.

'Omigod, Issy! You look awful.'

I told her the story of the eye, in full goryfied detail, elaborating upon reality by adding in some hair-pulling and then ending the horrifying episode with:

'A hazard of the job, apparently.'

'Thank God, it wasn't me,' she squealed. 'But you'll never guess what?'

'What?'

'We just got another gig and some studio time.'

SURPRISE, SURPRISE

Max made me a get-well card. He can draw an almost decipherable face, a lopsided circle with two inner eye circles, a circle for a nose and a wonky line for a mouth. Pretty good likeness, considering my present state.

Then at home further delights lay in store: a blinking answerphone, a rare occurrence these days. Pressed play and was rapt by the dulcet tones of Stephan asking if I was free on Friday, for dinner.

A Date
Was I free
Yes Yes Yes
As a bird
But
Fuck
Hideous eye eye eye
Another time

See, I'd called him straight back.
'I'm leaving on Saturday for the States. Don't worry if you can't make it.'
'I'd love to but . . .'
I ran through the eye saga.
'So I should book somewhere dark and atmospheric.'
'Perfect.'
Dug his sense of humour. Ha Ha Ha.
'Pick you up at eight?'
'Great.'

Dearest Almighty God,
Me again! First off, can I just say how amazing you've

been to me recently. I still have my job and my neighbour is alive. Thank you so much, I really do appreciate it. I have been trying to be a better person, and, well, actually, the other day, I did my friend a big favour by working her shift but, as a result, I now have a swollen bruised eye. I realise in the scheme of things this isn't such a big deal, but I also have a date this coming Friday. My first proper date in an embarrassingly long time. So I guess what I'm trying to say is – God, can you fix it for me? Please? I mean I know beauty is only meant to be skin deep, but the date in question is with a man. So let's be realistic here. God, make me better.

Thanks for listening,

Issy.

DISTRACTED BY THOUGHTS OF STEPHAN, TWIDDLING THUMBS (oh yeah, baby – just there) AND ABUSIVE MALES (harder . . .).

Just for the record, I hate filing (Stephan pressing his lush lips against mine in a passionate embrace). The office system had almost reached meltdown. With the best of intentions I took everything out, had a good old rummage (mmmmmm . . .) and then ended (astride Stephan, his hands gripping my breasts as I . . .) putting everything back exactly as was.

Trisha was much impressed with my apparent diligence. We were back on monosyllabic speaking terms, until, that is, a near hysterical (aghh, Jesus, this feels good . . .) Mrs Bob Thornton called saying (no no, hold back . . . then shifting position to take him . . .) she was going out of her mind, having found yet another email, though (he lifts me and kisses me, bears his full weight down upon me and together in perfect harmony . . .) in the trash can, i.e. not sent.

Trisha calmed her down and told her to send it through. The email read: (post-coital sweet nothings) 'Trixi bitch, I hate you after what happened. You're just one big prick-tease. Slag.'

'So it seems Bob was at the gig?'

Bob was hanging round my neck, like a loose noose, and what with the eye, the impending date, the gathering emotions, I flipped. Near hysterical breaking point.

I screeched, 'He wasn't at the gig, Trisha. He wasn't there. Ask anyone, ask Nadia.'

'OK, OK.'

'It was your case to begin with. I was only meant to be helping out.'

'OK, I hear you, I'll sort it out. OK?'

'OK.'

I was shocked by her conciliatory stance. I was shocked by my emotional outpouring. Sooner or later it was bound to happen. The truth would out and I'd lose my job but now, what with the threat of closure looming, I was hanging in there for a decent redundancy.

CALL ME RELLY, CINDER RELLY

Dreamy Stephan sat opposite me at a corner table, lights dim. The swelling of my eye had subsided, but the bruising hadn't. It was camouflaged beneath layers of delicately applied foundation. So much for keeping the faith. Nadia turned up at mine to babysit – a favour returned – and I had until 1 a.m. to seduce this man and get him between my sheets.

Mid-course in a Primrose Hill restaurant and he was

much amused by my job. Was I cool, relaxed? Not on your nelly. Jesus, but my stomach was in rag order, could feel my tummy-control knickers biting, was sweating pig-fashion and gulping back as much red vino as possible. Also made the fatal mistake of ordering a garlic-saturated starter.

Nervous in case the eye put him off, I, casual as possible, spent most of the evening with the left side of my face in the palm of my left hand. Man, I was so out of practice: dick dates were nothing in comparison to this.

Stephan was dressed in a crisp white shirt and blue jeans, having just taken off a black jumper. I was sucking up whiffs of his deodorant, imagining his broad chest beneath, the type you could lick, tongue nudging into each and every crevice.

'Sorry, what were you saying?'

'I was going through Sarah's personal stuff.'

'Oh Christ, don't tell me you found your mother's vibrator?'

'Pardon me?'

'Nothing.'

'Was that a joke?'

'A feeble attempt.'

Wince, wince.

'No, I was wondering what I should do with it all.'

'Give it to charity, I suppose.'

'There's so much, it's overwhelming.'

'I'll help you go through it, if you want.'

'You would?'

'Sure.'

The waiter arrived with our main courses, and as we tucked in Stephan continued on the same theme.

'There seems to be so much organising to do. How do you dispose of a grand piano?'

'Maybe donate it to a music school or any school.'

'Great idea. I put her apartment up for sale today. I'll have to return to deal with all of this.'

Ohh . . . so he was going to come back.

Thus there was the possibility of a long-distance love affair: how romantic. I gushed, excused myself and went to the toilet.

It was half-eleven by the time we'd finished our coffees. I was tipsy and merry, my confidence alcoholically bolstered, but the undeniable fact was we hit it off. I was getting that good-vibe thing, and we linked arms, zigzagging the short distance back home.

His apartment approached first and we paused outside the door.

I played the man.

'Can I walk you to your door?'

And further . . . if I play my cards right.

'You're one funny lady,' he said, pulling me close into him.

'Funny ha ha or funny weird?'

'Bit of both. Want to come inside?'

'Thought you'd never ask.'

See, we were on the same wavelength.

RESULT

We were making out. It was a quarter to one and he'd only just touched first base, due to getting waylaid by a whisky or two – error in retrospect – leaving a mere ten minutes to make a home run and relieve Nadia. Second base. I so needed this, my eyes rolling in their sockets, fingers on his zipper . . . Hey, come out, come out, wherever you are. Aha, got you. Doing my utmost to coax him further, and then at the strike of one, the bells ringing out, there I was crying, 'Come on, get a friggin' move on, I'm running out of time here.'

OK, so it was the wrong thing to say. Put it like this: Stephan didn't respond so well under pressure.

ONE DEFLATED EGO AND I

Just my friggin' luck. Two people steeped in embarrassment. Reality always falls short of fantasy.

Pissed off and pulling my clothes back on.

'Great!'

'I swear that's never happened before.'

'Yeah, right, and don't go blaming it on my hideous eye.'

'Come to think of it, it was kinda offputting.'

'Stephan, I really have to go.'

'We could always go back to your place.'

'Max is there, he's bound to come in . . .'

'Guess I got to be up at five. Got an early flight to catch.'

He was trying to make light of a shite situation, which induced instant sobriety, and the realisation that we were two people who hardly knew each other.

Politeness descended.

'Better luck next time, hey?'

He walked me downstairs and out on to the street.

'Thanks for tonight, Stephan. Pity it had to end so abruptly.'

'I'll be back in a month or so.'

A rushed kiss, one last smackeroony, and then he waved me off as I, with my lower half aching so bad, dragged myself home.

* * *

Of course Nadia saw the funny side of things.

'Why didn't you ring – you could have stayed out longer. There's a really good movie on.'

What? But! Whimper, whimper.

There was no way I could go back for seconds – way too desperate. Even I have limits.

Nadia got out the emergency supplies, a tub of choco, double-fat-saturated, sad-singleton carton of ice-cream, while I rolled a spliff.

We pigged out, we smoked, she left and I went to bed.

I mean sometimes you gotta do things for yourself.

I was so sick of doing it for myself and then, interrupted, I heard the familiar plod, plod of Max on his nocturnal wanderings. I relish these nightly visits into my bed. My little time marker is growing way too fast and will, soon enough, find cuddling his mum a gross turn-off. That's the way it is, I suppose, and by that time my hair will have turned grey and my fanny caved in.

Harbouring such thoughts, I sobbed into my pillow.

The 'Woe is me' floodgates opened.

I'd probably have to go back to counselling.

PINK PUFFERY

Then I heard this small voice whispering through the darkness.

'Are you OK, Mum?'

'I'm a little sad.'

'Why?'

'Sometimes people get sad.'

'Why?'

'Can't be happy all the time.'

'Why?'

'Things don't always work out. Like that time when we went to the park playground and even though we'd only just arrived, the woman was closing it and you got really upset.'

'Why?'

''Cause it was winter and they close the playgrounds early. So we never got a chance to play.'

'Mum, did you not get to play?'

'Not for ages.'

'You want a cuddle?'

My heart was disintegrating, and though I'm not one for romanticising motherhood, there are melting moments of bliss that sweep through you, a love that is staggering in its impact, phenomenal and fundamental.

In short, it's the answer to the question why.

LIFE STINKS

Another Monday night at the Honey Trap.

Fiona caught me mid-yawn, feet up on the desk and listening to *The Archers*.

'You look busy.'

What could I say, but, 'I've already done the filing.'

She pointed to a pile of post I'd been ignoring. I sprung into envelope-opening action. I hadn't seen her in a long time, not since the Bob episode. She'd put on a little weight, those sharp masculine edges rounding off.

It was deathly quiet, no new leads, no dicks pending, not even a Bob email to occupy me. Thus Fiona kindly set me a list of painful, irksome tasks to do, including updating her address book, sorting out the clothes in the emergency cupboard and checking stationery stock-levels.

Whilst I busied myself, she watched. When sufficiently bored, she put on her 'Melanie Speaks', an audio guide on how to talk like a female.

'One word men use more than women is "want". Men "want". Women don't "want", they "like" things. They "would like" things.'

'Fiona, don't tell me you actually believe this,' I smirked.

'Shut up, it's interesting.'

'A guy will go to a fast-food restaurant and say, "I want a Big Mac." Whereas a woman will go, "I'd like a small salad, please."'

'Fiona . . . it's total rubbish.'

The male in her still dominant, she turned the volume up and totally ignored me.

'Women can have moods . . .'

'OK, that bit's true.'

'But they can't have opinions. A man would say, "I'm going to do this," whereas a woman would say, "I was thinking I ought to do this," meaning, "I'm inclined to, but if you have any objections I'll reconsider." To feminise your voice stay away from assertive words, and use the "kind of, sort of" words.'

'As if,' I groaned, having a grand aversion to such stereotypical crapology.

Fiona switched off the machine.

'OK, enough of this. Issy, d'you want a coffee?'

'Mmmm, I'd like a cup of tea.'

'Have a coffee, don't be so difficult.'

'Oh all right then.'

'Got you.'

She pointed her finger at me and burst into affected peals of girlish laughter.

I grimaced back at her, thankful the green light began blinking, and reached over to lift the receiver.

'Hi, the Honey Trap, how can I help?'

'Oh hello, er.'

My caller sounded nervous, a little bit anxious, all perfectly normal in the circumstances.

'Mmmm you do . . . you er, test out . . . I mean set up . . .'

'That's right, madam. Are you considering using our service?'

'My husband and I, we've been married fifteen years and I have a feeling, looking back on things, it's struck me –'

'He may be seeing someone else?'

'Quite, but, to further complicate things, I think he may be gay.'

'Oh . . .'

'So I was wondering if you have any male decoys?'

'Hold the line, please.'

This was a first.

I put her on hold and signalled to Fiona to take the call. I'm not sure what would be worse in the rejection stakes: discovering your husband was gay or that he was having an affair. It's all too confusing – sometimes I reckon it won't be long before we evolve into self-satisfying hermaphrodites. Either that or we'll clone ourselves as the opposite gender.

Fiona took the call.

'Unfortunately,' she explained to the woman, 'in this instance we won't be able to help, but the Honey Trap is hoping to expand and cater to those precise requirements. If I could just take your number . . .'

The Honey Trap turning down work? Something

weird was happening to Fiona. She handed me a coffee and sat back down.

'I'm getting the snip, Issy, it's official. The appointment has been made,' she said, flicking through some letters.

'I noticed your hair had grown.'

'Issy, I'm having the chop.'

'But short is more masculine. I think your hair suits you as it is.'

'I am having my operation.'

'What? Your operation?'

'Yes, it's imminent. Very shortly I will be as nature intended.'

'Isn't that kinda subverting reality?'

'Exactly.'

'Are you nervous?'

'Issy, do you get that smell?'

'Huh?'

I sniffed, nothing untoward unfurling in my direction.

'I seem to have been followed by a bad smell all day. I thought it was the hormones I'm taking. They change your body odour.' She was sniffing her pits. 'No, it's not me. I'm sure I smelt it over by the kitchen.'

'I'll check it out.'

Up I got and popped my head round into the kitchen.

'Yeah, I get it now, but it's coming from over here.'

A strange smell was emanating from the doorway, though not from outside. It seemed to be coming from the coat stand.

Nostrils flared as my nose approached the target.

Fiona's beautiful coat hung draped off a peg.

The smell stemmed from the coat.

Or to be more specific from the hemline of the coat.

Oh dear Christ.

As it wasn't caked in shit I had a feel and . . .

Remember the finger? It must have slipped through the lining and . . .

'Fiona, I think I know what it is.'

'What?'

'I think something is rotting in the lining of your coat.'

'What exactly do you mean?'

'When was the last time you wore it?'

'Today's the first time in ages.'

'You mean ages, as in the night I borrowed it?'

'Yeah, the night I opened the fridge and found the fing –'

We looked at each other; we looked at the coat.

Fiona started screaming.

'Issy, get that damned coat out of here!'

'What do you want me to do with it?'

'Now!' She was dry-retching. 'To think I've spent the day walking round with a decaying human finger in my coat. Get it out.'

Of course after I extracted the finger, I had the coat dry-cleaned.

Fiona didn't want it back after that. Looking at it only made her feel sick.

And that's how I came to own the beautiful black coat.

Finding the decomposed finger unleashed within me a strange sense of optimism. The finger provided a means to several ends: the end of guilt on my part, having lost it in the first place. For Sarah, well, she could finally rest in one piece. For the investigation, it was a prime piece of evidence. And finally, I confess, it could aid my desire to conquer Mr America. I would call Stephan and triumphantly declare, 'I found it, your mother's finger!' and he'd come post-haste over to my side. The abrupt ending of our last encounter would be forgotten, forgiven, glossed over, and we'd go at it like rampant rabbits. Oh yeah, almost forgot, and then he'd declare undying love, and we'd all live happily ever after.

Wishing my life away as Max does, convinced at present he is four and stretching his arms up over his head, to reinforce the point.

'No, Max, you're nearly four.'

'I'm four.'

'Nearly four.'

'Three and four.'

'You can't be two ages at the same time.'

'You can!' he declared defiantly, 'I'm three and four,' before storming out of the kitchen and into the sitting room where he immersed himself in his current obsession, Bey Blades.

See, the business with Stephan niggled, and being female I took his failure to perform personally. I'd mulled over the scenario a zillion times. Had my eye really put him off? Had I been too pushy, forceful? Was my seduction technique due for a revamp? (I guess, in retrospect, 'Sock it to me, big boy,' is not the most seductive of mating calls.) Perhaps I should have played the girly card more? I tried to fantasise about us but ended up back at the same point. Deflated.

Sometimes I wonder if I couldn't somehow manage to make a living out my neuroses. How perfect would that be? If I could just package all my anxieties and then offload them in a financially viable way.

'Mum, are you listening?'

On the phone, having our ritual catch-up chat. Me, baring my soul to her and all she could do was scoff at my predicament.

'Mother, can you be serious?'

'Issy, I don't know . . . do some performance art or something.'

'What, don my black leotard and tights and express my emotions through movement?'

My mother and I were struck by the same mental image. Yes, we both remembered that painful moment. I was twelve, pudgy, and on the precipice of puberty – and I don't think I'll ever forgive her for allowing me to make such a colossal prat of myself. It was the school's Christmas variety show, and I was naive and centre stage, dancing, or rather 'physically emoting', to . . . wait for it, 'Bohemian Rhapsody'. The audience laughed. It wasn't meant to be funny. I swear it was one of the most cruelly humiliating moments of my life. I fled the stage in a complete state of shock, only to be dragged on again to uproarious applause. Afterwards my mother consoled me, promising that by the next day everyone would have forgotten it.

My whole school career was blighted by that incident.

'So what happened to the finger?'

'Damn detective. I mean at the least you'd have thought he would have been grateful.'

When Fiona booted me out of the office, I'd handed

the finger in to the police station. Bambuss wasn't there, so I'd left it with the duty officer and that was that, no acknowledgement, no thank-you call, no nothing. So much for being the good citizen, for being a responsible, law-abiding, honest person who pays their taxes, toes the line, keeps to the kerbside but in a middle-of-the-road sort of way.

'Oh and Freddie sends you and Max his love.'

'Sorry?'

'He's here at the minute.'

'Christ, like he could have told me. How long has he been there?'

I could hear my brother grumbling in the background, pretending he was me.

'He arrived last night, it was a spontaneous decision, and don't be horrible to him.' (Who, me?) 'He's feeling a bit down.'

'Oh boo hoo, poor little lambikins.'

'Issy!'

'Well, make sure he brings me and Maxy back some good presents.'

Sod, wish I could jet off to sunny New Mexico at the drop of a mood.

WHERE'S THE PAYOFF?

God,

I have a complaint to make. I'm doing my best down here, and yes – I admit there was some personal sat-isfaction derived from finding the finger, a sense of achievement, but the fact is, I'm not wholly satisfied with my lot. There, I've said it. I have this feeling of being short-changed all the time, like I'm missing out on loads of things. Well, like having fun, for instance. OK, I'll be more specific. The ability to lose myself in a moment, to not know what's coming next. To find a sense of freedom within the boundaries of motherhood. All this routine stuff – it sometimes feels like I'm wading through the days. Oh yeah, and I haven't had any of those flying dreams for an age.

Are you certain you're looking out for me up there?

Issy.

UNDER SURVEILLANCE

Unbelievable as it may sound, the glamorous world of Honey-Trapping is not always what it's cracked up to be. Many of the dicks I come across live up to the name and, of course, it's not all bars, bistros and booze. A lot of the time is spent waiting, an activity I am not particularly good at.

My next mission was to test my capacity for boredom. His better half sought out our services because she was anxious (see, it's not just me!). There was something amiss, probably not an affair, but something was definitely wrong.

She explained, 'Jonathan is of a generation where being emotional or opening oneself up is considered to be unmanly.'

'OK, so he's anywhere between twenty and eighty.'

Not a bit of it, he was a fifty-three-year-old solicitor. A mild-mannered, well-turned-out, well, gentleman. My mission was to tail him for a few days. He had been working late, a lot. Same old, same old, but you can never be certain, a lesson learnt on one of my early assignments.

FLASHBACK TO: WHEN FIRST IMPRESSIONS DON'T COUNT

I'd thought it was a clear enough case, having espied my dick verbally canoodling with another woman. Let's call him D, 'cause I can't remember his name. He had a suit job and I would loiter outside the firm and then tiptoe in his shadow, watching his every move.

One evening, after leaving his office in the City, he took a slow stroll from Fenchurch Street over the river to Waterloo, a good couple of miles, only to end up in the Goose and Fox, a non-descript working man's pub. He hadn't clocked me – after all, I was clad in black (mama mia, mama mia!). I waited outside for a while before entering. When I did, he was with a young woman. They sat at corner table chatting, and it was clear to me that this meeting had been prearranged. I noticed how he touched her hand, how he leant in to catch her words. She played with her hair and would look directly into his eyes: there was definitely something between them.

What else but a young mistress? Chuffed with my detecting skills, I assumed I had the case wrapped up.

D's wife came by the office the following day and I broke the news to her as gently as I could.

'Is she pretty?' she sniffled.

'Not a minger but she'll never be a model.'

'And thin?'

'Not a grosser, size twelve-ish?'

Unfortunately his wife was a good size eighteen.

'And . . . and how old?'

'Much younger than you. Twenty-five or thereabouts.'

She began sobbing, deep, throaty, heartachy sobs.

I really felt for her and asked Trisha to take over. Trisha does empathy and compassion so much better than I do. Guess it's because she's a divorcee and could relate more.

Anyhow, it turned out I'd misconstrued the whole scenario. The woman was his daughter, the result of a fleeting affair with his landlady, a year or so before D had met his wife. Having had no prior knowledge of her existence, to his credit he welcomed her into his life. And so did his wife. It was a rare case for the Trap, in that it had a happy and humanly uplifting outcome.

This experience taught me not to be so presumptuous and eager to jump to conclusions. Reality doesn't always match one's rational logic. All of us are apt to prejudge: being a single mum is a prime example. When pregnant with Max I thought how cool, what an adventure. I had no negative feelings about doing it solo. It was quite a shock to learn that having a child alone does not garner you with social kudos, the stereotype being a young woman, strung out, benefit-dependent, of loose morals, uneducated, who spends her days in front of the TV, dreaming of being on *Jerry Springer*.

STILL WAITING

The past couple of hours had been spent at the Church of the Holy Trinity, Brompton. Not for the benefit of my soul, I hasten to add. It was mission work. Jonathan Taylor's nocturnal wanderings were restricted to a brisk stroll from his office to the nearest praying house on the Brompton Road. There he would stay for the evening service. It was all very tedious. I remained outside, on the steps of the church, dressed as a Romanian gypsy. It worked a treat, I was conspicuously inconspicuous and even managed to make a bit of money. However, when the real McCoy turned up, I'd had to abandon the pitch. So having shivered my arse off, I then tubed it home only to find –

SANTA MARIA AND GOD GIVE ME STRENGTH

Outside the flat, I screeched to a halt and rubbed my eyes in disbelief.

In plain view (hadn't yet got it together to replace the net curtains, top of the list for the past few weeks) where anyone could have seen them, were – get this – Maria and Bambuss. Yep, the babysitter and detective were sitting on my sofa and he, our very own cor-blimey Columbo, was gingerly kissing the tips of her fingers. The tips of her fingers! I noted a bottle of wine on the coffee table.

Come again.

Listening to the friggin' Fugees – hadn't played that CD for ages – and then he made his move, went for the lunge.

One time . . .

An outrage, I tell you. I wasn't having that.

Two time . . .

Oh for Chrissakes.

And who'd have thought?

Their lips within millimetres of touching.

I surveyed this tender moment, grossed out yet voyeuristically captivated. Hands cupped as binoculars, pressed close to the glass, the gravel giving way, bush rustling, and then, the siren shriek from Maria when she glimpsed me Tom-peeping. Next thing, she was reeling off a list of saints I'd never heard of, and Bambuss jumped up, as if ready to balance out my bruises.

'It's me,' I yelped.

'Issy! What you doing?'

Excuse me? I could well have asked the same of them.

Three sets of eyes sent pinball-whizzing. I didn't know where to look, didn't know what to say.

Maria gulped and mouthed, 'You gave us such a fright.'

Likewise.

'The Detective and I . . . We were just . . .'

I raised a flattened palm. After all, we were all adults.

'Issy, you back early. I didn't expect you,' gasped Maria.

'Clearly,' I countered.

She was in a right old fluster, puffing up the cushions, while Bambuss pulled on his navy double-breasted blazer and then had the audacity to say, 'Taken to begging, Ms Brodsky? I could arrest you for that.'

Very funny . . . Not. I threw him a stinker of a look. Besides I was truly miffed that I was the only one to have not yet got my leg over on my own sofa. I mean why the hell was he in my apartment in the first place? I'd made it clear to Maria that boyfriends weren't welcome.

He left shortly after, though not before thanking me for the missing finger. Better late than never.

'So how's the case going? Caught the culprits yet, Detective?' I queried.

'Let's just say we're following up on some interesting leads.'

'Hmm, well, do keep me informed. In times such as these it would be novel to see justice done.'

THE LITTLE MINX

Maria put on the kettle and we settled ourselves down to a little inquisitioning.

Arms crossed and eyebrows raised, I demanded a full explanation.

She duly complied.

'He knock at the door, and I say you working and he say, I want company?' (What a smooth operator.) 'Issy, sorry if you are disappointed in me.'

Disappointed? I was jealous.

'Maria, exactly how long has this been going on?'

'Nothing is going on!'

'Not from where I was standing.'

'I swear, it was first time. My stomach so full of butterflies, I thought I'd burp one out.'

'Oh my God, tell me, tell me, spare no details.'

'Issy, we talk about everything, everything, and then he say . . .'

'What?'

'He say, I think you beautiful.'

'Me?'

'No. Me.'

'That's so romantic.'

Come to think of it Stephan hadn't said anything like that to me.

'And then he took my hand and . . .'

And all the while I looked at Maria thinking Max had a point, as she, at that very moment, was seventeen and fifty.

Having watched Maria whizz off into the night, so visibly glowing that she outshone her reflector belt, I realised anything was possible. I mean, she and Bambuss, though not exactly over the hill, were teetering on the summit, and well, there I was in the very prime of my life.

Yep, a prime time to call Stephan. Seize the moment and all that, 'cause in truth I'd been dithering, waiting for the right time, mood, astrological line-up. Jeez, maybe he'd forgotten me. Yeah, definitely time to remind him of my existence.

'That's right, Stephan Bloch.'

'Hold the line, please.'

Dum dum twiddly dee.

'I'm sorry, Ms Brodsky, but his line is occupied.'

Shit, and this was after my fifth attempt and two glasses of wine.

'Look, it's important I speak to him – does he have voicemail?'

'Would you like me to put you through to his personal assistant?'

Now, she offers me his assistant. I mean it wasn't like I was selling double glazing.

'This is Stacy. How can I help?'

His PA sounded hyper-efficient, terribly busy, and this made me nervous.

'Oh hi . . . I'm Issy Brodsky, a friend of Stephan's. I'm calling from London and was wondering if you could put me through to him.'

'Stephan's out. May I take a message?'

'Well, it's quite important. It's of a personal nature. I was hoping to speak to him directly.'

'Would you like me to take a message or not?'

'OK . . . could you say that I have vital news regarding his dead mother's finger and could he give me a call as soon as he gets this message.'

'What's your number?'

'He has it.'

'In case he doesn't.'

Hark at Miss Snooty, so direct and to the point and someone I never wish to meet face to face. She made me feel I was taking up valuable telephone-line time.

'So, you'll tell him it's really important?'

'Yes.'

'And can you emphasise the really?'

'Thanks for your call.'

'Oh, OK, well –'

She cut me off in mid-flow.

WHERE WAS I?

Deep in pending and if there's one thing I hate it's when people say they'll call and don't. Worse still is the fact you know the call ain't going to come but harbour a smidgen of hope. I hate smidgens of hope, so disappointing and slight.

So very disappointing.

Stephan never got back to me, and forty-eight hours later, my mind was spiralling. I highly suspected Stacy hadn't passed on the message. Probably fancied him herself. Christ, maybe they were having an affair, maybe they were doing it over the desk when I rang.

I kept busy, anything to distract myself, and indulged in some long-overdue spring cleaning. There I was, going through my young man's wardrobe and filling bags bound for the charity shops. Ah bless, but don't they grow so quick! Rummaging through his pants drawer I was discarding his Bob the Builder ones, as he now favoured Spiderman. So enthralled was he with his new kacks that he'd taken to wearing four pairs at the same time.

Fiona Apple was blasting in my eardrums, me being so in the mood for some female angst. I'd already given away most of Max's baby stuff, like the cot, pram, baby bath, crib. It had been a poignant moment, acknowledging that the likelihood of having another child in the near future was slim. I'd gone through a phase of wondering why women bothered to have children, considering the sacrifices one has to make. I'm unconvinced women can have it all: the man, the career, the kids. Something's got to give. Unless of course they're wealthy enough to have full-time nannies.

Being a special agent and looking after Max, I really don't see how I could ever find the time to fit in a decent relationship.

Yeah right. Who am I trying to kid?

And as for having another?

The fact is nature pulls so damn hard. I swear it's primal. The internal egg timer just keeps on running. I've already made a note in my diary that when I hit thirty-six I should get a few eggs frozen. When Max turned two, my body was ready to go at it again. Mid-cycle was hell – it was as if my insides were rebelling against me for not giving them what they desired. OK, so I'm not exactly an earth-mother type, but I concede there are times when I'd love another little being to nurture. Such moments are, however, transient. The thought of having to go through the whole baby thing again is wholly unappealing. All that selfless giving has severely depleted my coo factor. On sighting a newborn, I tend towards the 'Aghhh!' rather than the 'Awwww . . .'.

Damn, why hadn't Stephan returned my call?

I was tempted to take a break from my chores and dial again, but held myself back.

I could do aloof.

Besides, it was the middle of the night in La La Land, as the security guard kindly informed me.

Duh, did I feel stupid.

OK, so I could do aloof, if I tried really hard.

Distracting myself was proving rather difficult. God damn it, but why didn't the phone just ring?

And on that note it did.

Power of positive thought, hey – but how wrong could I be?

'Hello, may I speak to Issy Brodsky?'

'Speaking.'

'Hi there, it's Julia from the nursery office. Now don't get alarmed but Max has had an accident.'

'Oh my God. Is he OK?'

'He's fine, but –'

'What happened?'

'Really, he's fine.'

The call every mother dreads. The thought of my boy being in pain is excruciating.

Julia continued in her sing-song voice.

'It seems . . .'

(I hate such words, so very vague.)

'It appears he was playing with another child when a fight broke out over a ball, and the other child hit Max on the face. He's had a nose bleed and as it bled for quite a while, we're a little concerned and think maybe you should have him checked out in Casualty.'

'What? Who did it?'

'It was one of the other children.'

The nursery adheres to a strict policy of not giving

128

out the assailant's name, in case distraught mothers seek revenge.

'What was he hit with?'

'A wooden toy car.'

'Christ . . . I'll be there as fast as I can.'

Poor Maxy. I raced to the nursery, swift as my legs could carry me, guilting about leaving him prey to other people's fucked-up kids. It truly grates that he should have to suffer for another child's psychological problems. What's worse was that I knew who the kid was, 'cause Max had been coming home with bruises galore of late and had been bitten. You do your best to arm them with confidence and then some little vomit knocks it out of them. And I know it's the way of the world, but . . .

CONFESSION

I am a victim/survivor of a biter. Yes, it's true. I can remember, even after twenty-five years, being led into the toilets by a certain girl and allowing her free access to my four-year-old arm, to munch on. It wasn't a one-off, indeed it became a sort of ritual. I can't recall when it ended – maybe it coincided with an outbreak of warts on my inner elbow. In retrospect that sounds about right. Jesus, and come to think of it, maybe it was she who had given them to me in the first place.

'Max!'

He was sitting in the corner, quietly reading a book.

'Max, what happened?'

When he saw me he started to cry. I lifted him up into my arms and covered him in kisses.

'Are you OK?'

His nose was swollen and there was a gash across his cheek.

'What happened, Maxy?'

The teacher regarded me sympathetically, pushed an accident form into my hand, then started on about the incident with the other 'child', but Max set her straight.

'I was playing with the ball and David' (Aha, I was right) 'wanted it. I said no, and he said you're a donkey head and hit me with the car.'

I could see David in the corner and so wanted to fling it straight at him but . . .

'That's a nasty thing to do. Did he say sorry?'

'Yes, but now he's not my friend.'

With friends like those . . . and the worst thing was, Max appeared more upset about David not being his friend than about his sore face.

'These things happen,' smiled the teacher inanely.

'Yeah . . . whatever,' I replied.

We sweated it out in Casualty. No bones broken, so it was fine, but I bore a grudge and mentally struck through David's name on the list for Max's next birth-day party.

MY REAWAKENING

Spring sprang upon us and flowers peeped shyly out of the hard soil before being plucked to death by Max. There seemed to be a universal sigh of relief as light flooded our afternoons, stretching the days out. The grey backdrop of the city changed to light-grey and everyone appeared uplifted in spirit. Everyone that is, except Mrs Taylor.

After two weeks of tailing Jonathan (the religious freak), I'd come to the conclusion that he may well have been suffering a personal crisis or a spiritual reawakening but he wasn't seeing anyone.

'I find that hard to believe,' his wife sighed, her lip scrunched up tight at one side.

'I can assure you, Mrs Taylor, every evening was spent deep in prayer. I witnessed him with my own eyes.'

'Then why, Magdalena' (my aptly chosen name for this mission) 'has he asked me for a divorce?'

My answer was I hadn't a clue.

'Magdalena, he's in love with someone else.'

'God.'

I shook my head in genuine disbelief.

'I don't require flippant sympathy.'

'No, I mean he must be in love with God. So I guess the one thing you have in your favour is that you exist . . . tangibly, I mean.'

Magdalena.' She regarded me with an overly large amount of disdain. 'No, you see, he's in love with his junior partner.'

It transpired they'd been having an affair for three years. She too was married, which meant their activities were restricted to between nine and five. (Phew, at least that was me off the hook.)

'Jonathan said he was finding it intolerable to live with himself, and me, and now wants to marry her.'

'I'm shocked, really. I don't know what to say. How did you find out?'

'He confessed.'

Hence the soul-searching. At least my work wasn't completely in vain. I watched the tears well up in her eyes and motioned to Trisha to come over and rescue me.

Peeved to the nth, I couldn't believe I kept getting landed

with dud dicks. My scores on the board had gone into negative and Nadia won the monthly bonus yet again. Straight up I confronted Trisha and asked if there was a conspiracy against me.

'No.'

Her abruptly negative reply, tinged with a certain amount of cynicism, wasn't in my mind credible.

'Yeah right, I know all about back-stabbing office politics.'

'Issy, sometimes I feel really sorry for you,' she snorted.

'Thanks,' I replied, 'cause this time the tone of her voice rang true.

BUT THE GOOD NEWS WAS . . .

Stephan called. Mr America done good. Never doubted he wouldn't. Guess he was playing hard to get.

'Issy, this a good time to talk?'

It was after midnight. The phone had pulled me back to consciousness.

'Stephan?'

'Sorry, I know it's late.'

I yawned loudly.

'I was asleep.'

'You want me to call tomorrow?'

'No, it's fine.'

Besides which, I was awake.

'I got your messages.'

Note, he said plural.

'It wasn't a social call,' I blurted out, just so he wouldn't think I was gagging.

'Aw, shame, 'cause I've been thinking about you.'

'What were you thinking?'

OK, so I was gagging.

'Honestly?'

'Yeah, I can take it.'

'Well, I was thinking you're a real sweet lady.'

What the fuck does that mean? Sweet as in insipid? As in little sister, as in yeah, she's nice but I wouldn't have a relationship with her?

'Is that a compliment?'

'Sure is.'

'I like compliments.'

'You have any for me?'

Wish I could have said yeah, you're a great lay, but unfortunately I couldn't. I did the next best thing and replaced his sweet with:

'And there I was thinking what a nice man you are.'

'Nice?'

'Sweet?'

We were level-pegging and then he said, 'What's so urgent you rang ten times?'

'Nine. I'll show you my phone bill when you're next in town.'

'My assistant said it was really important.'

'I found your mother's finger.'

'I know.'

'You do?'

'Uhuh. The fat detective told me. Issy, I have a favour to ask.'

'Pray tell.'

As ever, I was open to suggestion. Oh, how I love to tease.

'Remember, you said you wouldn't mind helping me with Sarah's stuff?'

'Did I?'

OK, so where was this heading?

'Well, I was wondering if you'd keep an eye on the

apartment for me. I'd really appreciate it if you could pop in, put some fresh flowers in a vase, air the place, that sort of thing. I can wire you some money.'

Come again?

'It would be a really great help. I'm hoping it will sell soon.'

'Oh.'

'Would you mind? And of course if there's anything you want, feel free to have it.'

'Like the grand piano?'

'Maybe not the piano. I dunno, books, clothes, records. But please don't feel obliged.'

'Eh . . . OK.'

There I'd been hankering after a more romantic type of proposition.

'Thanks, Issy, you're a doll. I'll call the estate agents, get them to give you a set of keys.'

Surely I would be doing a good deed in helping Stephan? Plus, it would further serve to impress the Almighty that I truly was on my way to becoming a better person, a giving person, and one deserving of finding a mate.

Stephan and Issy.

You must admit, our names went well together. Though I wondered why I pined after someone who lived across the Atlantic, and with whom previous experience had been so disappointing. Was it the challenge? The fact that it was so unlikely to work? His inaccessibility? No, none of it, to cut the pseudo analytical psychology, it was the sad fact there was no one else and life's just so much more palatable when there is daydream fodder to mulch over.

I'd be out of there pronto – it's the cowardly streak within. Since Max's arrival, I'd only ever had skirmishes of the heart, nothing as substantial as a deep and meaningful relationship. For the first two years of his life it really wasn't an issue, but now Max doesn't depend on me so much, I have time to pursue the possibility. Working at the Honey Trap hasn't helped either. All I witness are crap relationships, heavy with insecurity, inequality; ones where, to be frank, the woman is always the loser. The thought of trading in my independence for a life of continual compromise ain't awe-inspiring. Still, what I'd give for a heart flutter, a little ping ping . . .

PLONK

Peter Branson was pouring me a glass of red. Yep, back at work and on another dick mission, with Nads. Peter was an accounts manager for an advertising company, thus socialising was a big part of his job. Soho House was the venue. Peter was easy to spot, being six foot two and sporting a trendy mullet.

We found him on the top floor, sitting with clients, all boys. It was easy to infiltrate the group. Nads and I, placed a little distance away, spent half an hour passing glances till we were asked to join their table. One guy latched on to Nadia real quick, a Frenchman who was very cute, and who, if the circumstances had been different, I wouldn't have minded myself.

My job was to focus in on Peter. Early thirties, successful, he mentioned his wife every second sentence, which translated to me as a clear signal to back off. I marked him down as incorruptible. Here was a genuine good guy, a family man. We ended up talking about kids, and it was obvious he was mad about his own.

When I announced I was a single mum, his reaction was one of gracious admiration.

'You're brave. It's hard enough with two parents.'

'How does your wife cope?'

'Poor thing, suffers dreadfully from post-natal depression.'

Cue for the conversation to open up. Nadia took centre stage, the men quizzing her about the band, which made me feel like the ugly mate, so I butted in with my Gonad joke. It fell flat and I finally had to admit it wasn't funny. Though Peter did raise a corner of his upper lip, but only to let out a plosive burp.

By the third bottle of champagne, we'd turned to the topic of midriffs and pop singers. Yep, Nads was still under the spotlight and baring her flat honey tum. The guys all wanted a yank of her piercing. Shame, I couldn't join in: my protruding belly hung over the top of my black jeans. Very soon I was either going to have to go on a diet or admit I was a size twelve.

The evening continued until Nads, having come back from the toilet, announced we really should get going, babysitters and all that. Peter suggested sharing a cab, my place being on his route home. How gallant, I thought, and so we black-cabbed it. The conversation returned to domesticity, the importance of family, etc. A perfect husband sat at my side, though unfortunately not mine.

I joked, 'Peter, if you should ever get divorced . . .'

Again it bombed and he looked kinda horrified.

Then, well, I did something I probably shouldn't have. It was clear he was a hundred per cent kosher, and I felt I needed to save face, so I came clean about the situation.

'Look, your wife obviously needs reassurance, otherwise she wouldn't have called us.'

His reaction was one of utter astonishment.

'Excuse me?'

Then changed to one of disgust.

'Wait . . . Nadia and you . . . You're telling me this was a set-up?'

'I wouldn't worry – you passed with flying colours.'

'What a fucking bitch.'

I assumed he meant his wife.

'Well, she is depressed.'

'What?'

'Your wife, you said she was depressed.'

We sat in silence till the cab pulled up outside my apartment.

I had an ominous feeling I'd landed myself straight back in the shit again. Blowing your cover whilst on duty was deemed as sacrilegious as blowing your dick. Placing the dick in such an awkward position makes for an irate customer, unwilling to foot the bill, and shifts me back a pace into the position of job on the line. Which let's face it wasn't a great distance.

Will I ever learn to think before I speak?

'Look, Peter, I really shouldn't have said anything.'

He put his fingers to his lips and sneeringly said, 'I won't say anything, just as long as you and your "friend" Nadia don't.'

I staggered out of the cab and limply waved him off.

Shit and double shit.

Called Nadia the minute I'd managed to oust Maria off the comfort of my sofa and out into the cruel night.

'Nads, I think I may have fucked up again.'

'What do you mean again?'

Oh yeah, I'd forgotten she didn't know anything about Bob.

'Nothing, it's just, I let slip it was a set-up.'

'You what?'

'It kinda just came out. Well, he guessed.'

'What do you mean, guessed?'

'OK, so I thought he was a nice guy, genuine. I mean he really loves his wife.'

'Issy, he was a complete sleazer. He had his hand on my knee most of the evening.'

'Really?'

'Yeah. Didn't you see him put his little finger in my belly button? And he gave me his card, "Let's do lunch" scrawled on the back, kiss kiss.'

'But at the club he was –'

'Issy, he couldn't take his eyes off me. Didn't you notice?'

'Nadia, what am I going to do? There's no way we can tell his wife.'

'Why?'

'I sorta made this deal with him. He wouldn't tell her he knew it was a set-up and I'd say he was a great husband, because that's what I thought he was.'

'Issy, are you asking me to collude in this nonsense with you?'

'That's precisely what I'm asking. I need my job.'

'What about his wife?'

'She's depressed. One more thing could send her over the edge.'

'Issy, she's depressed because she suspects her husband of cheating.'

'Semantics. Please, Nadia. I made a mistake. He so blatantly didn't fancy me, and I thought –'

'He wouldn't fancy anyone else?'

Ouch, that hurt.

'It's just – I tried hard to impress him.'

'And I was thinking it was a clever ploy on your part, playing the desperate singleton to get him to notice me.'

Did she really say desperate?

I thought I was being cool.

'No . . . I . . .'

'You didn't think. Fuck it, Issy. Let's speak tomorrow.'

My brittle ego fairly shattered, two steps forward, one step back, seems like I'm inching my way down a hot-coal-laden path. A change of direction required.

No matter how hard I tried to put a spin on my life, it just wasn't going as planned.

SAVING ONE'S ARSE

By exposing it with head buried, the ostrich way. In plain English, I hid out in Sarah Bloch's apartment, away from the phone, ignoring the mobile and submerging myself in another's life. OK, so I'm a nosy bugger and was sniffing through her wardrobe. A bit like rummaging through your mother's, as a kid. Flashback to me in my mother's wedding dress, wading about in her high-heels, or those Godawful hippy skirts with tiny little bells attached.

Spent the entire morning dressing up. In the main it was old-lady stuff, twin sets and such, but there was a whole load of cashmere jumpers and a few dated ball gowns. She'd probably kept them as souvenirs of times past. One was a seventies dress, halter-necked, A-lined and deliciously vile, with a vomit pattern that swept down to the floor. Retro gold so I swiped that pronto. Another was a floaty chiffon number, very Pan's People. On alert my heart-beat, in case the estate agent walked in unannounced and found me in my underwear, or worse, my altogether.

I put aside a few more pieces of clothing and then began sifting through her shoes. Sarah was into shoes: silver, gold, mules, wedges, strappy sandals, boots, some with matching bags and belts. I opened the bags and discovered bits of tickets from years back, opera, ballet, concerts, dance, bus tickets; notes with numbers, gloves, even hard-boiled sweets (they tasted fine to me), coins, hairgrips, boxes of matches from restaurants.

On my knees, my grubby little paws Narnia-bound, I reached further into the wardrobe past the fur coats and extracted a hard-edged object, or box. Aha, what have we here, my hearties? Hidden treasure, dust-laden. I carried it out into the light. A secret box, mahogany, heavy, inlaid with with another wood. Maple? I wasn't sure. I placed it on the bed and lifted the lid. A thousand secrets lay hidden: OK, I exaggerate, it was full of old photos and scraps of letters, but there at the very bottom was a girl's diary. Here was free access to the innermost thoughts of a teenage Viennese girl. I could get it translated, the first few pages anyway. Imagine if she turned out to be the next Anne Frank? Here was a project to immerse myself in. I'd been on the look-out of late for a hubby, oops, Freudian slip, hobby.

EVEN KEELING

The next few weeks passed uneventfully: nothing un-toward. Work was bearable, no mad missions, just an average Joe whose wife was using us to boost his flagging confidence. Freddie showed up looking fresh from his recent jaunt and arrived laden down with goodies. Max was thrilled with his bag of the latest Disney toys and I was chuffed with a couple of DKNY T-shirts, a Prada shirt, and a pair of Seven jeans. My brother is the only person I'd ever trust to buy clothes for me. He'd done good then treated us to lunch at Wagamama's.

Still unattached, he began complaining about not having had sex for three weeks.

'I'm going crazy, it's killing me. I just don't think I can take it.'

'Get a grip. Three weeks is nothing.'

'What are you talking about? It's the equivalent of three years in gay time.'

'Earth calling Freddie.'

'Don't take the piss, Issy. Do you think I've put on weight?'

'No.'

Sometimes I wonder if he is aware how much he winds me up. My brother has a body to die for, is gorgeous, has some amount of brains, which he tends not to use, and the incredible knack of rubbing in just how boring my life is at present.

'You, though, have definitely put on weight.'

'Thanks, bro.'

'So I was wondering about liposuction. Maybe we could get a family discount. What d'you think?'

'I think it's unnecessary. If someone loves you they'll accept you, warts and all.'

He flinched, remembering the attack of genital warts that had massacred his social life for months the previous year.

'Bitch,' he fumed, fanning the menu in front of his face, and then turned to Max to declare, 'I don't know how you put up with her!'

However, his sulky mood quickly dissipated with the arrival of a terribly cute waiter. Quite the charmer,

Freddie switched to predatory mode and by the end of the meal they had exchanged numbers.

Bastard.

He called me after their first date, saying the guy had an absolute whopper.

Double Whammy Bastard.

And after the third date, that he was in love.

AS FOR STEPHAN

Thoughts of him continued to fill my mind. It was like I was experiencing a sense of nostalgia for how it might have been, if only our date hadn't been so crap. He called a couple of times, and we had long conversations that never seemed to go anywhere. I told him about the box, and that there were loads of baby pictures of him.

'Very cute, Stephan.'

'Wonder if there's any of my father?'

'Maybe.'

And I promised to have another peek.

The property market was experiencing a slump and no offers had been made on the apartment. He said there wasn't much point in coming over till then. I did manage to lure one male over my threshold but, seeing as he was a Jehovah's, it didn't really count. Nice enough though, very enthusiastic and spiritually inspiring.

When he left, I appealed to the Lord to deliver unto me a male, and on the double.

G man, hast Thou forsaken me in my hour of need? Or are you just a big teaser? But seriously, I'm ready, and well, the fact is, Holiest of Ones, the weather's on the upward turn and I'm longing for a bit of –

DICK DICK DOCK

After all there was a spare going.

Indeedy, for Fiona had gone for the chop and come out a new woman. Christ, I hope she knew what she had let herself in for. I'd warned her, it wasn't all lipstick and high-heels. Then again, she'd have it fairly easy, wouldn't be blighted with monthly cycles, nor the possibility of getting pregnant, which, let's face it, is a major part of being a woman. I'd always thought that, in her efforts to be female, she tried too hard. Her idea of what a woman was came from a male point of view, but still it tended towards a pastiche vision, i.e. either vampish or going for the mumsy look, just never normal.

You are who you are, whether you lose a leg or get a cosmetic makeover. Your psyche will remain the same. Though maybe that will be the next scientific breakthrough. People will opt to improve their person-alities, discarding therapy in favour of brain surgery: let's zap those synapses. Criminals will be targeted first. They'll be sentenced to lifetimes of being goody-goodies. The rest of us will cotton on, offering up our scalps, hoping to be reprogrammed: no more negative thoughts, anxiety, insecurity, depression, stupidity. There will be a choice of A-, B- or C-type personalities. (Yo, Doc, give me ambition with a high IQ and a confident, positive outlook, purrlease.)

Fiona once admitted to feeling trapped in the wrong body. I could relate. There were times I felt trapped in the wrong life, but I wasn't going to slit my wrists to spite my face.

I went to visit her in hospital. Propped up by a ridiculous number of pillows, she was watching an old

Bette Davis black-and-white movie from the bed. I'd popped by after having had another fight with Nadia, who remained in a right old huff about Peter. I'd left her chewing the cud. Having admitted I'd fucked up, I begged her not to blow the whistle on me. If she were to say anything I'd lose my job and did she really want that hanging on her conscience? Especially considering she, at least, had a budding other career, whilst I would probably end up a loser thirty-year-old serving friggin' lattes in a shite caff down the road.

Little bit of emotional blackmail never goes amiss. Heck, it works nine times out of ten.

'So how you feeling, Fiona?'

'Good. The bandages come off in a few days – can't wait to have a fiddle.'

'Yeughhh . . . too much information.'

'Well, you asked.'

'So how are you peeing?'

'A catheter.'

'Oh yeah, I had one of those when I gave birth to Max. Weird, isn't it?'

My nether regions frozen with an epidural – it was just the strangest non-sensation.

'Are you sore?'

She nodded.

'A little – it was really painful at first.'

'Sounds a bit like giving birth – except in your case, Fiona, you just rebirthed yourself.'

As a kid, a boy once whispered to me conspiratorially that fannies were just inside-out willies. And for years, I'd believed it.

'I like that,' smiled Fiona.

'So, do you feel any different?'

'Like I've come home.'

TO ROOST

Cock a doodle, Easter upon us and my little chick was flying around the coop, or rather whizzing up and down the hallway on his new scooter. Grandpa was over for a week, which had me in a right old flutter. Yes, that latent childhood desire to impress one's parent and prove I was successfully coping with everything reared up. He, on the other hand wasn't coping. His trial separation from his second wife was turning into a divorce. Malika had met someone else, and finally my father was beginning to appreciate what it was like to be cheated on. It hadn't helped that the man in question was an employee of his and younger.

Max was in his element and lapped up the male attention. He wanted to show his grandpa off to all his friends at nursery, and demanded my father take him and pick him up. Of course I was delighted, but it also illuminated the gaping hole in Max's life where a constant male figure should be. More guilt for me, and out with the cat o' nine tails.

As for my dad, he very sweetly suggested I pretend he wasn't here.

IF ONLY!

In my father's desire to make himself useful and not get under my feet, he managed to do just that. Tidying was in effect hiding things, and sorting was flinging out all my chipped crockery, though at least he had the decency to replace it. Worst of all though were those probing questions, which always niggled.

Like:

'Have you met anyone, Issy?'

'No, not yet.'

'It's not natural. Try the classifieds.'

'I'm not desperate.'

'How old are you now?'

'Drop it, Dad.'

'And the job, where's it going?'

'Dad.'

'Have you thought about a school for Max?'

'Dad, Dad, what the . . . Where are Max's sticks?'

'I threw them out.'

'You what?'

I was livid, having gone into Max's room only to find his entire collection missing.

'Issy, it looked like a heap of rubbish.'

Max was an avid collector of sticks. He began his collection when still a mere babe. No park excursion was complete without bringing home a twig or two. The boy loved sticks, he breathed sticks, sticks were his everything. What can I say, but that he had at least a couple of hundred sticks in an ever-growing stack piled in the hearth of the fireplace in his room. Many were labelled by me, detailing date found, where and use of.

'Max will go crazy.'

'Issy, you're overreacting.'

'We'll see.'

Later that afternoon my father went to collect Max, while I fretfully paced the apartment, expecting to hear anguished howls coming from way down the road.

But no, in skipped the boy, all breathless, his little face smeared with chocolate ice-cream.

'Mum, Mum, Grandpa is going to stay for ages.'

'Wha' d'you mean?'

Appalled at the thought, I looked to my father for an explanation.

'If it's OK with you, I wouldn't mind spending another week or so.'

'Please, Mum, please, please?'

God, I said a man, not my dad.

Yet . . .

How could I deny my child precious time with his grandpa?

I stared straight into Max's eyes.

'Max, Grandpa threw away your stick collection.'

'Ow, it was an accident.'

'Max.' I pointed directly at my father. 'That man destroyed your life's collection.'

'It doesn't matter, Mum.'

I was in a no-win situation.

'Oh, OK then,' I grumbled. 'Grandpa can stay.'

LIVING WITH MY DAD BY ISSY, AGED THIRTY AND A QUARTER

My father had decided to take time out, a sabbatical of sorts, an 'I can't deal with the world at the moment'. I kept him busy by introducing him to my garden, which badly required tending too. He rose to the challenge and provided me with a gardener. Not exactly what I'd had in mind, though the woman was really quite creative, given the space, and left me with several flowerbeds and a herb garden.

However, the primary advantage of having my father stay was free babysitting on tap. It caught me unawares and I was at a loss as to how best use this time. Having cultivated friendships with other mothers, I found they weren't very receptive to my proposal of going out, with a view to getting laid, as they were all in partnerships. Nads was either busy, rehearsing or working, Fiona wasn't quite yet up to going on the razzle dazzle, Maria was in lurve and Trisha claimed she was too busy. Freddie deigned to bring me clubbing, which was a mistake, as his nights out don't begin till the a.m. and getting totally mashed isn't conducive to good parenting. I ended up doubling my hours and as luck would have it met Joe Jones.

CUE JOE — HE WAS A LAUGH-ISH

Or maybe it was the way he told them. An accounts analyst by day, Joe was a budding stand-up by night. Dina his wife wasn't convinced of his comic genius and to be honest I'd have to concur, though I'd give him ten out of ten for trying. My mission was to attend all his comedy gigs and determine whether he had potential or was using it as a front to have a quick fling.

And so I found myself going to various open-spot nights across the city, the Purple Turtle in Camden, the King's Head in Crouch End, Mirth Control in Islington, the Fitzroy in Soho. Never knew there were so many clubs, but that's the great thing about living in London, there's always somewhere you haven't been to or something you haven't done. Watching these up-and-coming comedians I was struck by two things: a lot of them were attention-seeking neurotics, and maybe this was something I could do.

It's rare you find yourself in an environment where you feel completely at home, and I did. Humour has a viral quality about it, a bit like catching a cold. To witness a whole room reduced to tears of laughter by a punchline was inspiring, not to mention a release. Jeez, but I must have offloaded months of built-up stress.

I passed myself off as a wannabe, hung round after the shows and played the carrot, sucking up to Joe, just to ascertain if he was a dick. Naturally he was partial to flattery, as is every man, but declined to nibble.

Dina was relieved by my prognosis. However, pregnant with their first child, she was feeling emotionally insecure and wondered if I wouldn't mind continuing 'babysitting' her hubby. For once I was happy to oblige.

THEN ONE FINE MORNING

Mrs O'Whatshername greeted me full of her usual good cheer.

'Oh it's terrible, terrible,' she lamented.

'Hi, Mrs O' –'

'It's tragic is what it is. Have you heard?'

'Oh God, don't tell me, the neighbour upstairs has had a relapse?'

'What? No, he's in fine fettle, not a bother on him.'

'Phew. Listen, I'm late for a dental appointment, we'll catch up later.'

My annual dental appointment. Sitting in reception, wading through the classifieds, one caught my eye. 'Seduce and Destroy: The Honey Trap seeks new recruits in the war against infidel-ity [sic]. Are you discreet, charming, attractive, curious? Ring Trisha on . . .'

Now call me paranoid, but no one had told me they were looking for fresh blood. I mean it wasn't as if business was booming. I lagged far behind on the monthly scoreboard, so adding one and one together I came up with 45, as in P, as in mine.

TIME FOR A SHOWDOWN

Swaggering into the office, I thrust the paper down on Trisha's desk. She was plucking her eyebrows, going for the high-arch look, and flicking tweezered hairs all over the place. Hands on hips, I demanded an explanation.

'Eh, er, eh, Trisha, eh, I notice you're looking for new recruits,' I spluttered.

'Yeah, we are.'

'Oh, OK.'

I've really got to be more assertive, more . . . well, just, more.

'You wouldn't make us a cup of tea, would you, Issy?'

'OK.'

In the cubby-hole kitchen, I mustered up the confidence to then nonchalantly enquire, 'So how come you're looking for new staff?'

My voice was a tad shaky but I think I got away with it.

She ignored me and cried aloud, 'I don't believe it.'

'What?'

I was hoping she'd plucked straight through her arch, resulting in a gap.

'The care worker, did you know? It was the care worker.'

'What are you talking about?'

I handed her a mug and she pushed the copy of the *Camden New Journal* back into my hands. Jesus Christ.

There on page three was a picture of Bambuss, under the heading: 'Detective Fingers Care Worker'.

Ughh, poor Maria!

I mean, I couldn't believe it. Bambuss, a lothario, ye gads, but I guess beauty is only skin deep, then again, he is well wide of girth.

But no. Three columns dedicated to the valiant Bambuss who solved the mystery of the missing finger.

Three columns . . . and not single a mention of me.

In a case that has sparked much interest, Detective Christopher Bambuss yesterday announced that a formal arrest had been made. Sarah Bloch, 79, the renowned concert pianist, resident of Belsize Park for twenty-five years, was robbed only hours after she passed away. The thieves, not content with a swag of more than £50,000 worth of antique jewellery, had also hacked off the victim's finger to remove a precious-gem ring.

I skimmed through the rest of it.

The pair were named as Mark Sawyer, 23, unemployed, and Bernadette Quinn, 45, care worker.

'The care worker. Can you believe it?' Trisha had started on her stray chin-hairs. 'You managed to keep that one pretty quiet, Issy.'

'The care worker,' I repeated, stunned by the revelation.

AND OH HOW HE ROUSES ME

Damn, but there's too many fucked-up people in this city. You put your trust in someone only to be royally shafted.

'The care worker, and her junkie boyfriend.'

Stephan woke me once again. I told him it was becoming a bad habit.

'So exactly how long have you known?'

I was playing the pissed-off girlfriend.

'A while. I thought you knew.'

'I can't believe you didn't tell me,' I moaned.

Jeez, but this role came easy to me.

'Can't believe you didn't know.'

'Well, you could have told me. Huh.' (Allowed a pause for a sigh.) 'So are you coming over?'

'Soon, finally getting some interest in the flat. There's a couple of viewings this week. If you want you can suss them out for me, act as my spy?'

'Why would I want to do that?'

'So you could choose which neighbour you'd rather have.'

'Oh yeah.'

I hadn't thought of it like that.

THE CONTENDERS

On behalf of the vendor, it was only right I established exactly what type of person the buyer was. Oh my but he was delicious, devastatingly handsome and divorced. Hurrah. And had a child. (Sunny days are here again . . . Max and I, each having a new best friend, scenario already envisaged and the guy had only stepped over the threshold.) Very charming, Jon, without an H, a doctor – now you're talking. How handy would that be to have a GP on tap – not a GP, 'I'm a plastic surgeon,' oh excuse me – even better! (And already I was feeling five years younger.)

Yabba yabba and please, fingers crossing, even toes, please, please, buy the apartment, there I was extolling the virtues of the area.

'Yes, I am very interested' – great – 'Thanks for all the info, lovely to have met you.'

Bye, bye, lovely to have met you too, and now, Mr Estate Agent, who's up next?

An elderly couple.

Sharp blast of buzzer, someone impatient to get in, and I heard a high-pitched voice screech, 'Hello? Hello? Are you there?'

Strangely the voice sounded vaguely familiar.

The estate agent opened the door and there stood the Finklesteins.

Gladys, whom I'd never met, stood next to Joel. Desperately I tried to summon up superhuman powers that would allow me to vanish into thin air. There is nothing worse than meeting a client on the outside, especially considering how risible our meeting had been.

Gladys Finklestein, small and plump with dyed red hair, was wearing a J.Lo tracksuit and heels. She extended a hand heavy with gemstone rings, and introduced herself.

'Isabel,' I replied, and then turned towards her husband. 'Hi.'

See, I wasn't sure if he'd remember our little incident, prayed he wouldn't.

'Have we met before? You look familiar,' he said.

'I don't think so,' I ventured.

153

'It'll come to me, it'll come to me,' and providing an echo, Gladys quipped, 'It always comes to him, it always comes to him.'

'Well, nice to have met you, but I really should be going.'

'I remember now!'

Joel Finklestein pointed an accusatory finger at me.

'You're the one from Harry's!'

Gladys Finklestein pointed a manicured finger at me.

'She's the one from Harry's?'

I nodded a confirmation.

'Yep, I am the one from Harry's.'

'The escort!'

The estate agent raised two brows at me.

'I'm not an escort!'

God, get me out of here, now.

In the end it wasn't so bad. Joel apologised for his discourteous behaviour, Gladys apologised for having booked me in the first place and I told them that the flat was really old and would need to be totally renovated.

'And you do know what happened to Mrs Bloch?'

They didn't, so I filled them in on how Sarah met her grisly end, embellished the facts a tad.

'The police say it was burglary but we all suspect it was murder – the area has really gone down. My son found her hacked-off finger in my garden.'

'Stop, I feel sick to the stomach listening to this,' wailed Gladys.

'Anyway, best to know these things.'

So I selfishly did my utmost to put them off buying the place, though purely on the grounds that contender No. 1 was male and available.

NEIGHBOURS – EVERYBODY NEEDS GOOD NEIGHBOURS

One evening on the way to work, I passed my upstairs neighbour.

'Hi there, you look nice,' he said, opening the door for me.

'I see your eye is back to normal.'

'Thanks, and the scar suits you,' I remarked, doing my utmost to repay his compliment. His fall had left him with a gash along the side of his left eye and temple.

'You're just saying that, aren't you?'

Feeling rather cheeky I couldn't resist the temptation.

'Yeah.'

I laughed.

'Off anywhere nice?'

'Work. What about you? In anywhere nice?'

And I was being facetious rather than flirty.

'Hmm, I'm waiting for my girlfriend.'

'Oh and I thought you were being gallant, keeping the door open for me.'

'No,' he replied, dead serious.

A little cough, an ahem, ahem, interrupted our tête-à-tête. I stepped aside to let his girlfriend pass.

Brushing by me, wearing one of those vapid false smiles, she looked me up and down and then with much smugness said, 'So you must be the single mother.'

MIMICKING THE RIGHTEOUS

'So you must be the single mother . . .' And she's like mid-twenties, high-maintenance, ludicrously pretty, totter totter in her heely-wheelies and – it was the way she said it, like it was derogatory. OK, so maybe she didn't mean it that way, maybe it just came out wrong, but I felt truly insulted.

I'd reached the office in a right old huff happy to see Nads and Trisha. If anyone was to understand how I felt it would be them, seeing as we were all in the same boat.

'Well?'

'You take things too personally,' sighed Trisha.

'Do not.'

'Do too – you make a big deal out of everything,' Nadia groaned.

'I can't help it if I'm ultra-sensitive.'

Their response? To laugh at me.

'Thanks, guys, most empathetic.'

Before I could go off on another whinge, Trisha silenced me and announced, 'I'm throwing a party for Fiona next week. Nadia says she'll sing. What about you?'

FIONA'S REBIRTHDAY PARTY

My first party in an age and I was intent on letting rip. As requested, I arrived early to provide a helping hand. The venue was Fiona's home, a maisonette in Chalk Farm.

Trisha whizzed round being hyper-efficient, Nads was practising her set and I, well, I didn't really do too much. Mainly, I got in the way, though being the person who just gets under others' feet is, I believe, a necessary role in the preparation of any celebration.

With only five minutes to spare before the first guest arrived, Trisha sank back in the sofa to appraise her successful transformation of Fiona's once chintzy home into that of a chintzy home with decorations. Chinese lanterns hung around the garden, which was half decked and half lawn. There were loads of floating candles in bowls of water, and large cushions strewn randomly. A special cocktail had been designed by a bar-tender friend, and there was lots of scrummy food on platters, buffet-style. Not the usual dips, olives and salads. Oh no, it was crayfish, crab, king-size prawn and rare beef something or other. It was catered, no expense spared, near on seventy people but way low on the hetero-male count.

I flitted amongst the crowd, quietly getting sozzled, when Leanne, a writer, introduced herself and then proceeded to give me a detailed account of her life history. Her problem, if you ask me, was that she over-analysed everything. Man, but she bored the tits off me. I was trapped in a one-way conversation, all about her, her, her.

Next thing was, she launched into a description of her latest opus, which, as far as I could make out, was, yep, all about her.

'Fascinating,' I yawned. 'You're obviously a very deep and complex person.'

I excused myself and escaped to the makeshift bar in the sitting room. Unfortunately so did Leanne and we stood mutely beside each other, waiting to be served.

I spied Nadia hovering on an arm of the sofa, talking to a pretty-looking guy. Trust her to home in on the only hetero male, and I made straight for them.

'Jesus, Nads, I've just met the most self-obsessed person of my entire life.'

'Were you looking in a mirror?'

'Excuse my friend. She suffers from an inferiority complex. Hi, I'm Issy.'

'Issy, this is Mack.'

'Mack the Knife? Bet you haven't heard that before.'

He smiled, crooked teeth, endearing rather than off-putting, and probably around my age. A couple more drinks and I'd consider him a viable possibility.

'Issy works at the Honey Trap,' Nadia sweetly informed Mack before vamoosing off to set up for her little sing-song.

Mack, an artist, had recently exhibited his paintings at a local library. The show, titled 'Colour Conscious', was, he explained, a comment on our multi-ethnic society. He painted different-sized canvases in different skin-tones.

'Cool. I've often thought I could have been an artist.'

'Really?'

'Yeah. A conceptual one. I had this idea I'd get a toilet roll and on each sheet I'd write the name of someone I'd pissed off. I'd call it 'Everyone I Ever Pissed On'.'

Mack didn't like my idea, opined it was derivative, and went off to talk to Leanne.

So I had another drink and then a couple more. The cocktails were lethal, they crept up on me slowly, then wham, like a sledgehammer, hit me full on, forcing me out into the garden for some fresh city air.

I slunk down on the edge of the decking, half hoping to disappear, half hoping someone would stumble over me. Nearby, Fiona was chatting with friends. Centre of attention, she looked fantastic, a bit like a dark-haired Jerry Hall (OK, so my vision was alcoholically affected). She was dressed in a figure-hugging red number that accentuated all her newfound curves and a fine pair of legs.

I spotted Bambuss and Maria and waved over to them. Maria was all made up, cheeks glowing and

cleavage showing. Bambuss had his arm wrapped pro-
tectively round her waist. He'd made an effort too, his
hair greased back, double shiny, and was dressed more
casually than usual in denims and a loose sweater.

'Issy, you not drinking too much?'

Maria leant forward to kiss me.

Wasn't sure how to answer that, so turned to Bambuss
to congratulate him on the piece in the journal.

'Great detecting, Detective, great piece, but it missed
a certain something.'

I was in catty mode.

'What's that?'

'A mention of me.'

'Ah, Ms Brodsky, of course.' He patted his left breast.
'But I think they edited you out. I told them everything.'

'Figures.'

Trisha did the honours, hushing the crowd, before
a nervous Fiona made a short speech, thanking all for
their support in her journey to becoming a woman.

My impromptu rendition of 'For She's a Jolly Good
Fellow' didn't catch on and Fiona continued, '. . . I'd
also like to thank the one person who has been my
anchor, my support, my true friend and partner and
whom I love with all my heart . . . Trisha, thank you
so much. I could never have done it without you.'

Nads and I clocked one another. Was this confession
time? So Trisha and Fiona really were a couple?

Overcome by emotion, Trisha began blubbing real
tears. Wow, Trisha had feelings.

So wished I'd brought a camera.

They hugged, the crowd cheered, and Nadia began
her rendition of torch songs.

'Issy, you OK?'

Trisha came and sat down beside me.

Drunkenly, I hiccuped a response.

'Do you think you're going to be sick?'

I shrugged my shoulders, too early to tell.

'So, Trish . . . is it true about you and Fiona?' (Wink, wink.)

'What! Don't be an idiot.'

'Bitch.'

I was rather inebriated, not nauseous but definitely obnoxious. I'd reached that stage where you can't control your tongue any more and all the shit you've stored up starts spilling out.

'Trisha, you have a real problem with me. Don't you?'

'I think you're drunk.'

She went to stand up but I grabbed her arm.

'Go on. Let's just clear the air. You can tell me to my face.'

Unfortunately at this moment I burped in hers.

'Issy, if you really want to know, I came over to say sorry.'

'For what?'

'I think I owe you an apology.'

'Why?'

'I came down heavy on you with the Bob Thornton case.'

'Oh, not that –'

'Yes, that. Look, I was very stressed and I realise I took it out on you. So, I'm sorry.'

'Aw shit.'

The over-emotional drunken stage hit. I threw my arms around her and splurged, 'Trisha, you're great, no, really I have to say that, I really, really admire you.'

Jesus, but my heart was pounding, I was puce in the face, on an adrenalin rush. The formidable Trisha had apologised to me.

Unheard of.

Unreal.

She was obviously as smashed as I was.

I was off the hook, could put that dirty little Bob episode to rest.

Torch songs over, the DJ started spinning tunes, and the garden heaved as we all reared up and let loose.

But see the thing was . . .

Ten minutes later, Nadia and I were strutting our stuff. Or rather I was jerking about rather haphazardly but jubilant in mood.

'Nads, I mean she actually apologised.'

'I told you, she's not so bad.'

'About Bob! She apologised to me. I mean it's such a relief.'

The music blaring as the pair of us fog-horned across to one another.

'Nice one.'

Thumbs up to me.

'Yeah.' Then I had to tell her, couldn't keep it a secret any longer. I leant over and drunkenly confided, 'But see, the thing was . . .'

'You shagged Bob!' shrieked Nadia.

This wouldn't have been so bad if it hadn't coincided with the music suddenly stopping and Trisha dancing within earshot.

Nadia looked at me aghast.

Trisha gave me the most vile stare ever, then slowly walked off.

'Oh shit,' sighed Nadia. 'Issy? Issy, are you OK?'

OK?

An understatement perchance?

No, I was not OK, I was far from OK, I was . . .

CAUGHT IN A NIGHTMARE SCENARIO

The call came through at 21.00, one week after the party. Big boss Charlie on the blower, requesting my presence, or else. I faltered, couldn't bear to pick up the handset. My heart went all tribal with a boom, boom, boom. I paced the long hallway, muttering under my breath, 'They're not gonna get me, they're not gonna get me.' And it occurred to me that maybe I could sue Tatu for breach of copyright, considering that specific phrase was my very own intellectual property.

Trisha was out for her pound of flesh. How vindicated she must have felt, her intuition correct all along, her bloodhound nostrils moist and twitching, face gurning in readiness to pounce on her prey, which was me, and rip it to pieces, nay, smithereens. Ever so slowly, with relish, her sharp, orthodontically whitened gnashers biting, tearing, would strip me of all human dignity and reveal me as the barefaced liar I was. A fraud, a liability, the weakest link.

'Goodbye.'

'No, Trisha . . . No, you don't understand.'

She came to get me in the deep dark night. Then, the next thing was she had me in a head grip, was dragging me up the stairs and into the office.

'I knew it,' she screamed, a woman obsessed. 'Traitor. Infidel.'

'Trish, mate, I made a mistake, a human error.'

'You think that's what Judas Iscariot said to Jesus?'

'Maybe, who knows? I wasn't there.'

'Don't get smart with me, young lady.'

'But maybe that's why Jesus said forgive others and not go casting stones about. Correct me if I'm wrong, but did he or did he not say "Turn the other cheek"?'

Head locked, I tried turning mine and my neck clicked. On the bright side Trisha may have inadvertently corrected that wayward vertebra back into place.

'Snivelling dog,' she barked. (I know, I know, an awful pun.)

The door of the office creaked opened and she flung me into total blackness. Gee whizz, but the gym thing really works for her.

Into a void, a big black hole of nothingness.

'What do you have to say for yourself, Brodsky?'

'Mummy, I want my mummy.' Yep, I truly did say that.

I was scrabbling about on all fours. She nabbed the nape of my neck, then with Hulkish strength, pulled me up and pushed me down into a chair. A mega-wattage desk lamp clicked on and shone directly into my face.

'Listen, Trish . . . I know we haven't exactly seen eye to eye, but don't you think you're overreacting?'

'Shut up. Rope, please.'

A shadowy figure emerged from the murky blackness. I recognised the silhouette as Nadia's. Damn, but she even looks good in monochrome.

'Et tu, Nads? Turncoat.'

And she called herself a friend.

'Sorry, Issy, I . . . She made me.'

'Yellow-bellied cowardy custard,' I hissed in Nadia's face.

It's weird the phrases that come out when one is under such extreme pressure.

'Shut up, Brodsky. Nadia, tie the bitch up.'

'Trisha, I swear I didn't do it.'

My last stab at denial, reckoned I'd nothing to lose.

'Playing schtum, hey? You can't pull the wool over my eyes.'

She slapped me hard across the face, which I thought

was uncalled for. Literally was struck dumb and couldn't think of a half-decent retort.

'Nadia, make sure she doesn't fall asleep. Keep the light shining till she cracks.'

'Ha,' I bellowed, 'I'm a mother, you dipstick, immune to sleep-deprivation.'

'Yeah, she has a point.'

In the background I heard a tape machine whirr and then, 'We have ways of making you talk.'

It sounded like Fiona. Kinda like a woman, definitely like a man.

'Trisha, it was just, a mistake, more like mutual masturbation. We were drunk, it was non-emotional, a slip of the –'

'It's too late for apologies, Issy.'

'No, please no.'

Jesus Christ. I watched as she reached into her trousers and took out a . . .

'Oh my God, Trisha, not that.'

A dick, I mean a penis, a male member, severed, and I blushed. Hadn't seen one up that close in an age.

She was jabbing it at my face.

And that's when I forced myself to wake up.

There is a limit to how far my subconscious will go.

MY FALL FROM GRACE – REAL TIME

Yep, I woke up and Max was flicking my cheek.

'Mum, Mummy, it's time to get up.'

What, what? Morning already? A quick glance at the alarm clock confirmed I'd overslept.

My father's face popped round the door.

'Thought we'd let you sleep in. I'll take Max to nursery.'

'Thanks, Dad.'

I hadn't mentioned my impending doom to him. My imminent sacking weighed heavy on my mind and he sensed something was amiss. The whole weekend had been shadowed in gloom, and I found myself snapping at Max for no valid reason. Being a confident kid he took it in his stride.

'Mum,' he stridently declared, 'I am nearly four and you are thirty. Do not shout at me!'

He was staring up at me and I could see he had a point.

'You're right, Maxy, sorry.'

On edge and waiting, oh, how I wished to put off the inevitable.

Crawling out of bed, I went to take a shower. I let the water pelt down, hoping it would somehow permeate my skin and cleanse my thoughts, only to be interrupted by the sound of an insistent bell. I cursed my father for forgetting his keys yet again, and wrapped in a towel sloped off to open the door.

'Jesus, Dad, but how many times –'

Surprise, surprise.

It was Fiona, clad in a very becoming Burberry mac. I have to say she's got good taste in clothes.

'Nice coat, is it new?'

'Brodsky, you and I have some serious talking to do.'

'We do?'

She nodded.

'Meet me at the café round the corner in twenty minutes.'

I complied, found her twenty minutes later in the café on the corner, tapping away on her laptop.

'Hey, great party the other night. Christ, I was so drunk.'

'Glad you enjoyed it.'

'Drank way too much, can't remember a thing.'

An inane smile graced my bullshitting, and desperately I continued digging a hole into which I might fall.

'Regret getting so drunk, always end up talking such shit.'

A surly-faced waitress intervened.

'What can I get you, ladies?'

We ordered coffee and cake. Then, just as I was nervously about to embark on recounting my hideous dream, Fiona hushed me with a flattened palm and opened her briefcase. Reached her finely manicured hand in and took out a file. Or rather, the –

BOB THE BANE OF MY LIFE FILE

And you wanna know something?

'Twas the sweetest sacking in all of Christendom.

Fiona went for the caring, motherly approach.

'Issy, you're a complete and utter tool.'

'Thanks, Fiona, the feeling's mutual.'

'What's that supposed to mean?'

'I think so too.'

She peered across the table at me, gulped back an espresso, reached out a hand, which she gently and ever so reassuringly placed on mine, then soothingly sneered, 'You're finished at the Trap.'

'As in –'

'Yes.'

Although she did say that if I wanted I could consider my situation as being on permanent suspension without pay.

'Can't say I'm terribly surprised.'

My tone was sardonic and I flicked her hand off mine. The last thing I needed was insincere pity.

'Issy, I feel I should tell you this. Normally, in situations such as these, people have a tendency to say don't worry, it's not personal. One mustn't take these things personally.'

'And?'

'Well, in your case, it was.'

'Excuse me?'

'Personal. Trisha always doubted you. Right from the start. She's been watching you like a hawk –'

'Fiona, you're the boss.'

'Trisha founded the company. The whole thing went belly up a couple of years back, so I bailed her out. We're equal partners. Anyway she thought you were, how can I put it, an encumbrance, bound to mess up. She thought you were using the position as an attempt at a social life.'

Whoaa there, matey, time to douse my tongue with a petulant fragrance and pretend I was a six-year-old, little Miss Precocious.

'Fiona, have you any idea how tedious it is to be fawned over constantly? It's actually quite distressing having all this male attention. OK, so I'll admit it was fun at the beginning, meeting people and going out, especially considering my situation, but frankly –'

'What?'

My voice pitched higher than usual and I threw in a lisp for effect.

'Well, if you must know, I've found these past few months borwing.'

'You mean boring.'

'Yesth, borwing. Look, Fiona, I want to move on in my life, achieve something worthwhile. I want Max to be proud of me, not embarrassed that his mother works as a spy. I mean can you imagine how that must make him feel? Especially as he starts school next year.'

'What are you talking about? Having a parent who's a spy is the ultimate for a kid.'

'Yeah, well, maybe.'

Damn her. I cut the affectations, they weren't working, and went for a plain old fuck-you attitude with a splash of moral high ground.

'Fiona, for all I care you can keep your scuzzy job. I mean why am I bothering wasting my time in a two-bit agency that deals in grief? That generates suffering. Let's face it, most of the guys are so bowled over by the fact an interesting person is talking to them it's no wonder they succumb. It's like giving a kid candy – they can't help but take a lick. It's deliberate provocation.'

'Issy, you're talking like a man. And by the way, may I remind you that these past few months no one was licking you.'

'That was a run of bad luck, and you know it. Honestly, Fiona, there are nights I'm actually unable to sleep, grappling with thoughts of the hurt I've caused others. We manipulate these guys. If the shoe was on the other foot, I mean if their wives had a chance, they'd probably jump at it too.'

'Business is business . . .'

'It's morally corrupt and you know it. It stinks, the whole of society is defiled, we're force-fed a diet of titillating sex and then expected to be monogamous saints. It's all bullshit.'

'What d'you mean?'

'I mean people expect dessert with every meal.'

'Sorry?'

'Expectations, expectations, expectations.'

'And?' she said, polishing off her coffee-and-walnut slice.

'They are unrealistically high. You can't have your cake and eat it.'

At this precise point in the conversation, the café erupted. The sound of plates smashing to the floor reverberated throughout and was followed by the waitress storming out from the kitchen area. Spewing most virulently God only knows what (though it was music to my ears), the owner, Silvio, a short, tubby Italian, appeared in hot pursuit of her. There followed a scene of passionate anger, much arm gesticulation and verbal sparring, until she untied her apron, flung it to the ground and left. Silvio cursed her vociferously and then proclaimed, 'I've had it with her bad attitude. She doesn't want to work, she think she too good to work in café. Is true what they say. When will I learn? You canna work with animals and children. My own daughter. Pah.'

He collapsed against the counter and beseeched the Lord above.

'What now, Mister High Flyer? Why so impossible to find decent waitress? Honest, hard-working, easygoing, not complicated, pretty, but smart, young woman who lives local. Flexible hours, the pay not so bad. Where? Where I find this miracle worker?'

HE PRAYED. I ANSWERED

Or rather Fiona nudged me into action, elbowing me in the ribs.

'Hey, over here. A perfect specimen ready to roll.'

'Fiona, what are you doing?'

'Sorting you out. Some things are fated to happen.'

'I'm an undercover agent.'

'Those days are long gone.'

'Rub it in, why don't you?'

'ISSY, IT'S OVER.'

Silvio rushed towards us and I flashed him a winning smile.

'Hi, mmm, I couldn't help but witness what just happened and, as I'm currently looking for a job, I wondered –'

'You have experience?'

'Some.'

Under the table Fiona's pointy-toed boot met with my calf.

'Loads,' I corrected myself.

I'd done a couple of waitressing stints as a student and vowed never, ever, to do it again.

'You good worker?'

'Let me vouch for Ms Brodsky. As her former employer, I can safely say she gives her all to the job. Perhaps at times too much.'

OK, so I was way overeducated for the position and felt it to be a massive come-down from the dizzy heights of undercover agent, but really, was I in a position to choose? I levelled with myself: it would be fine, for a while. A temporary measure taken to alleviate financial ruin. At least it would allow me space to look for a more suitable job. Silvio passionately embraced me and then set me to work.

On the bright side it wouldn't take long to master the art of serving and hey, waitressing, well, it's not exactly rocket science.

Jesus Christ, but have you any idea how bloody complicated a simple cup of coffee can become, how fickle a customer is, how demanding, rude and obnoxious people can be?

'Hi, can I have a coffee?'

'What colour?'

'Mmmm black, mmmm, no, white.'

'A latte?'

'No, a cappuccino, without the chocolate.'

'Anything else?'

'With skimmed milk, and an omelette.'

'OK.'

'But without the yolks.'

'Want any bread with that?'

'What sort do you have?'

'White, wholemeal, soda, baguette, ciabatta, rolls.'

'You have any crispbreads?'

'Chrissakes, Fiona, just make a blinkin' decision.'

Fiona was my trial customer. Silvio had thought it best to test me, just to ascertain my suitability for the position.

I managed to scrape through, though no thanks to Fiona.

WHERE ART THOU, FAIRY GODMOTHER?

She stood right in front of me, a little smaller than expected, but definitely of the fairy ilk with her pink tulle tutu, angel wings and a wand. Twirl that baton my way, babe. Instead she scoffed at me, her tiny nose upturned, and skipped away, waving her wand about her. I was contemplating my fate at the council-run Elysium, otherwise known as the playground. I'd picked Max up from nursery, and we'd headed over to the park.

I am so jealous of a child's sense of joy and freedom, the sheer ecstasy they derive from climbing frames, swings, and sandpits. These little people letting their souls dance are sovereigns unto themselves, still too young to be self-conscious. The children rule supreme in these safe havens, where the only knocks experienced are soft bruises and the niggling wounds of childhood, like from the kid who throws sand in your eyes or runs off with your tricycle, or clouts you when you're not looking, but in the main, bliss abounds. While we, the parents, guardians, hover on the sidelines, waiting for the tumble, the call for help to push the swing, to build the castle, to buy the ice-cream.

Speaking of which. Tantrum alert, tantrum alert, and there was no way his fingers would be prised from the railings. Max, steadfast and determined, clung to the rails on the far side of the playground, where the ice-cream van had pulled up, by the gap in the fence. The tingle, tingle tune that cuts to the bone of every parent and you just hope you remembered to bring your quid or all hell will break loose.

Of course being the parent who forgot, I hung back in the sandpit hoping no one would point the finger at me. 'Cruel mother ignores the pleas of her wailing child.' There was no way Max would be persuaded to forgo an ice just because Mummy had no money. So I decided not to deal, sat in the pit, and how apt a place considering my situation.

By rights, I should be an international lawyer, earning a fortune, married with two kids, a nanny and a 4 x 4. I should be living on the pig's back, given my education, upbringing, and the opportunities open to me.

Something went hideously wrong along the way.

Maybe I didn't suffer enough?

Jeez, but how I wish I was working class or at the very least belonged to an ethnic minority. I have zero credibility, no excuses, and blame my parents for making life too comfortable. Where was the struggle? The long haul out of the gutter? I mean no wonder as a kid I used to dream of being an orphan, like the girl in *Thursday's Child*.

OK, so I could get nit-picky and blame my vast array of neuroses on my parents' separation, but in truth, it's probably a reaction to having been raised in a pretty relaxed and nurturing 'right-on' environment; excepting for the fact that I wasn't ever allowed a Sindy doll or anything girly, was dressed in dungarees, ordered to climb trees and hence have a fear of heights. To be fair, my parents made loads of mistakes but on the whole have been very supportive: they helped me with my homework, urged me to go on to university, to travel, to take drugs and sleep around.

My sole attempt at rebellion was to become all religious in my early teens. I experienced a brief Audrey Hepburn nun stage, and had a crush on the male lead in *Jesus Christ Superstar*. It lasted three months, coinciding with the arrival of Ollie, the new boy in class, who made me melt, blush and burst into hysteric peals of nervous laughter all at the same time.

He also never gave me a second glance, and went for the biggest breasts in the class, belonging to a girl who used to charge boys fifty pence for a peek at her nunny during break times. I bumped into Ollie years later, on Oxford Street, wedged between sandwich boards, handing out leaflets. I scoffed at his lowly predicament and also 'cause he'd gone to seed and lost all his hair. Knowing my luck he'd probably be my first real café customer.

'Mum-meeeeee, Mum-meeeee.'

Max's screeches had become almost sing-song. And I wondered how long could I feasibly ignore him before one of us snapped.

Minutes? Seconds?

But hark, what's this?

The far corner fell silent.

Yes, respect to the man in the ice-cream van.

He must have caved in, taken pity on my poor deprived child.

As I brushed the sand off my clothes I could see Max licking a cone, sitting on one end of the small seesaw.

I went to join him.

'Nice one, Maxy.'

'Where were you?'

'In the sandpit. Can I have a kiss?'

'No way. Get off.'

He's already sussed my fake-kiss manoeuvre where I swoop down in the pretence of love and go for a lick.

'ISSY, WHAT ARE YOU GOING TO DO WITH YOUR LIFE?'

On the way back to the apartment my father's voice resonated in my head as I prepared myself for one of his lectures.

At key moments throughout my early life, I would stand in his study and he'd say, 'Issy, what are you going to do with your life?'

And I'd answer, 'Well . . . I'd really like to travel.' Meaning, 'Can I have some money?'

Or, 'Actually, I was thinking about . . .' Meaning, 'Can I have some money?'

Or, 'There's this amazing course, I just have to do it . . .' Meaning, 'Can I have some money?'

My father would contemplate my request, and wide-eyed I'd promise him I would finish the course this time, or take the job, or get my act together. He'd pontificate about how spoilt I was. I'd then exploit his sense of guilt for leaving us and ruining our lives. Next he'd throw his eyes to the heavens, I'd recant, say I was joking, give him a winning smile, and finally he'd write me a cheque.

There then occurred a change. A time when I did finish my degree, did get a job or a series of jobs and was getting my act together. Next up the Max arrived . . . and I have to say, becoming a parent has forced me to reevaluate my relationship with my parents. The role of a grandparent can be a vital and wonderful thing and not just from the babysitting aspect. I begged my parents to consider moving over to London. They both refused me.

'DAD, THERE'S SOMETHING I HAVE TO TELL YOU . . .'

'It sickens me. It truly sickens me. To think after all that money spent on education, all those course taken, then this should happen. A waitress! A goddamn waitress!'

In a rage, I continued on defiantly.

'Can you imagine how I feel? It pains me. No, really. I know you expect more from me and I expect more from myself, but it's hard with Max being so young and –'

My father laid down his *Financial Times*, peered over his reading spectacles and regarded me with an air of bemusement.

'Issy, what are you talking about?'

'I lost my job today, and then found another. I'm now a waitress.'

'And . . . ?'

'Well, it's outrageous, that I should descend to this.'

'Darling, it doesn't matter. Max is your number-one priority.'

'But you don't understand . . . If only I'd suffered.'

'I bumped into your upstairs neighbour today. He seems nice.'

'Why did you make it so easy for me?'

'Asked after you and Max.'

'You're not listening to me –'

'Interesting young man.'

'He has a girlfriend. OK! Look, all my life I just wanted to achieve something.'

'You have. Max. He's brilliant.'

'Anyone can be a mother.'

'Issy, stop beating yourself up. Who cares what you do?'

'What?'

'All I want is that you're happy.'

'Yeah, I suppose waitressing could be fun. I mean at the very least I'll get to meet loads of caffeine addicts. And you get tips, though not a lot. Silvio is a bit of a wild card. What's this?'

'Flowers. They were delivered about half an hour ago.'

A lavish bunch of flowers met my gaze, and when I say lavish this was not an understatement. My father had left them in the sink.

'Couldn't find any vases.'

Chief suspect was Stephan, and I ran to confirm my suspicions and examine further evidence of his lust. Aha, and there was a card peeking out.

'GET WELL SOON.'

I ask you. So I opened the card only to be greeted with: 'Best of luck in your new career. Trisha. Dizzy Issy, crazy babe, luv u lots, mis u alredy. Nads.'

She was currently going through a text-addiction phase.

'Thanks for all your hard work, Issy. The Trap will sorely miss your warped sense of humour. Take care and see you soon. Charlie/Fiona. Lovely Issy, I do cheap rates for favoured customers. Big kiss to Max. Maria. PS You have my number, use it.'

So that was it. It was over.

Finito, no going back.

'Dad, I think I'll go and get drunk, then curl up in a corner of self-pity and weep.'

'OK, lovely. I'll sit Maxy.'

DEEP IN SHITSVILLE

Seeking solace from a bottle of red wine shared with Nadia, who answered my plea as a true friend should and hastened to my side at Steele's. Soon enough I was infected with good cheer, encouraged by Nadia's optimistic outlook and general enthusiasm.

'Nads, you're the best friend I have.'

'Best and only one, by the looks of things.'

'Yeah.' My sozzled brain reaching fermentation point. 'So, superstar, wha's goin on with the producer bloke, geezer?'

'It's over.'

The producer, so very keen on her musical talent,

had turned out to be an arsehole supremo of the first order.

'How could I have been so naive?'

'You're too trusting, you gotta understand. They are gonna get you.'

'What?'

'Human nature, it's complex. What happened?'

Simon the schmoozer talked the talk and bigged her up. Oh but the promises he made, big deals in the offing, stardom awaiting, the glory to be had, but first. But first, let us retreat to my studio, he slimed, that being his studio flat, and snort a little cocaine and swill a little bubbly.

'What about the rest of the band?' an innocent Nadia had enquired.

'You're too good for them. I see you more as a solo artist.'

'You do?'

'A diva. An oyster pearl just waiting to be opened.'

She wasn't convinced but such was her desire to succeed.

And so Schmoozer lured her back to his pad and heaped compliments upon her. My, my, but such a talent. Here, have a CD or two or three.

'There's a track I'd really like you to listen to.'

Yawn, I'd been there, experienced saviours of the like, fallen prey to the manipulative male. How twenties, as in age.

'Nads, Nads, I expected more from you, what with your streetwise sophistication.'

'My what?'

So she'd ended up in his studio, freestyling over a track.

'Nice, dig it, babe.' And he transfixed by her youthful beauty. 'Let's have another drink?'

Intention being to ply her with booze, so she'd be all the more pliable, and loosen up those vocal cords.

'He could have doped me. Put something in the drink.'

She was right. Actually she was lucky. You hear so much about about date rape these days. Who would notice a pill fizz in a glass of champagne?

He'd laid a hand upon her firm thigh and had then begun to stroke softly in a north-south direction.

'What d'you think you're doing?'

'Come, come, Nadia. I've noted the way you've been looking at me.'

'You what?'

The schmoozer for all his efforts was gobsmacked. Our Nadia landed him one in the mush. Did I forget to mention her kick-boxing passion? How remiss of me.

'No one, but no one, takes the piss out of me,' declared a drunken Nadia.

I wish I had her sense of bravery. I probably would have succumbed.

'Jesus, I can't believe you did that. What did he say?'

'I didn't hang around to find out.'

We neared the end of the bottle and ordered another. Yes, I was feeling a million times happier.

'Nads, knowing your singing career has gone belly up has made me feel much better.'

'Issy, you're pathetic. But I know what you mean.'

We toasted our failures and future successes.

HA BLOODY HA

A week later Nads and I played the same scene, only this time at the Enterprise in Camden over whisky and Coke. She was doing her best to sort out my life.

'Issy, something will happen, it always does. Trust me.'

Abracadabra and poof! Through the smoky haze I spotted Joe Jones, the comedian.

'Oi!'

'Hi.'

'What you up to?'

'In general, stagnating, specifically, getting pissed. How about you?'

'Compering this night's gig, actually.'

Joe promised to fix our maudlin grins so that they upward turned.

He proclaimed, 'Ladies free before a certain bewitching hour.'

Up, up, we followed him up to a room above the bar. Found ourselves sitting in a makeshift auditorium. We counted six others, and took our seats.

'Tonight, ladies and gentlemen, it is our pleasure to introduce to you . . . Fanny Lipz – she'll crack you up.'

A ripple of applause ensued, then the spotlight turned on and a wee Scottish lassie bounded onstage, bellowing with much bravado.

'Hi, I'm Fanny Lipz and I'll crack you up.'

Sadly 'twas all hot air and Nadia slurred drunkenly, 'Issy, you could do better than that.'

'I could?'

'Sure, you got more more laughs from your heckle.'

'Open mike night, Thursdays,' winked Joe Jones, in my direction.

THE MYSTERIOUS MAN UPSTAIRS

I'm talking here about His Lordship, rather than my upstairs neighbour. The former amazes me and the latter has, over these past few weeks, become a morning regular at the café, along with his acidic girlfriend.

So, wonder of wonder, miracle of miracle, my having repeatedly issued celestial missives, doesn't the Almighty go and deliver.

Yep, under that grey cloud that was my life, there came a silver lining.

Morning shift in the café, Silvio in the kitchen, Max in nursery and my neighbour upstairs had just come for his usual strawberry smoothie followed by a latte.

'Hey there, Scarface,' I merrily chirruped, mindful of being extra nice to him because he gave good tips and also to annoy his girlfriend.

Never have I met such a whingey whiny cow. She complains constantly and is so obviously obsessed about her looks (which I'll admit are good, notwithstanding the amount of dosh she splashes on her face). However, my main gripe with her is her uncalled-for rudeness. She always addressed me in the most patronising of tones, looked straight through me, as if I was too lowly to register on her status scale of humanity. Realised she was probably incredibly insecure, and viewed every other woman as a threat. So I obliged, switched to agitator mode and flirted with my neighbour. Hence his nickname, though I have to suffer being called Nutter. All this flirting kind of embarrasses him though secretly I think he may even enjoy it.

Really don't get what he sees in her, bar the superficial, that is.

But hey, that's men for you.

So having prayed hard for some male interaction, the good Lord send that cheeky cherub my way. Bent forward, to clear my neighbour's table, tush up and out, then all of a sudden thwang went the bow, whirr went the arrow.

And I went, 'Oww, that friggin' well hurt. What the –'

See, I'd felt a pinching on my posterior. I spun around, ready to admonish the arsehole in none too polite terms.

'In the name of God, what do you think you're – Stephan?'

The very same, with a mischievous expression.

Stephan was back in the 'hood. Rascalian Stephan looking ever so hot, and bling-bling went my heart. 'Hey ho, hey ho, it's off to work I go.'

'Any chance of getting a decent coffee round here?'

Oh the voice just so does it for me.

'Maybe, though it pays to be sweet with the waitress.'

'Well, if you don't mind me saying, you're looking mighty fine.' He grinned. 'The eye thing cleared up real nice.'

'Cheers, and what is it you'll be wanting, cowboy?'

'A full English.'

Oh the subtext. I was all aquiver taking his order, had to hold the pen in both hands to make my writing legible.

'And a fresh orange juice, if that's not too much trouble?'

'No trouble at all, sir.'

I smiled my cheesiest grin.

'Good to see you.'

'You too,' he gushed. 'You look great – have you lost weight?'

One good thing about waitressing is weight-loss. You

can work up quite a sweat at lunchtimes and the coffee machine sure works those biceps. I was back in my pre-pregnancy clothes.

'A little.'

The return of my saint, and I just knew, from the way he was staring at me, I was in for a good time.

BUT NOT FOR LONG

In fact by the end of the day I was tossing and turning in Stephan's bed.

Thank you, God, for delivering unto me a most beautiful male, well versed in the ways of physical union.

My body awoke from a most long hibernation. In the café an unspoken something had occurred, a tacit understanding of what would come later. Well, me, for one.

A glut of emotions swept through me, bowled me over, brought me to my knees, and then some. Whooaa there, stallion, easy does it. Stephan was on a mission, like he'd something to prove to me. I guess he had, considering our last meeting.

So a couple of hours later, we were enjoying the requisite post-coital fag.

'Amazing staying power,' I ventured, all loved up.

'Issy, you're so sweet.'

'As Honey? Lost my job at the Trap.'

'I guessed. Don't tell me – you were screwing one of the clients?'

'Well, yeah.'

Excusing myself, I went to the bathroom. This could be it, we could fall in love and have a relationship, I was musing on saccharine notions as I tried my hardest to pee. My body, fair shook up, took its time, switching over to its utility function. Already, I'd chosen a pet name for Stephan, my Trojan Horse. How apt, how befitting, and I shuddered at the prospect of round two, unsure I could take it.

But damn, I felt so goddamn alive, vital, and then as I checked my appearance in the bathroom cabinet, just to make sure my make-up wasn't smeared halfway across my face, I noticed a packet of pills. I reached over and –

Well, well, what have we here?

I blinked in disbelief at that which affronted my gaze. So he did have something to prove.

Viagra.

My Lord, but you have a weird sense of humour. (Or am I just old-fashioned in wanting the real thing?)

I sashayed provocatively back into the bedroom, amused that Champion the Wonder Horse was in effect on pep pills.

'Hey, sweetie, ready for seconds?'

'What's the rush?'

I sidled up beside him on the bed.

'No rush, babe.'

'So, how long do I have the pleasure of your company?'

'A couple of weeks or so.'

'Mmm, fourteen long nights. I look forward to it.'

'Yeah.'

He coughed hesitantly.

'But eh, I guess I should tell you, Katy is coming.'

Katy? Who the hell was Katy?

'Oh great, it will be nice to meet one of your kids.'

I so didn't have a clue, half-clad in my underwear and climbing back on top of him. I began nuzzling his chest.

'No, my partner, Katy.'

'What, is she over for a case?'

So didn't understand.

'Not work partner, girlfriend.'

Thus instantly clarifying the situation for me.

'Oh, now I get it.'

I yawned, blasé-style, as if I didn't care that I'd just been shafted by a guy who needed a chemical dick splint to get it up.

What a bastard – couldn't believe I'd been duped. Why hadn't I seen it coming? Felt like a complete Nadser, i.e., a total idiot.

'Guess I'll make a move.'

I slid off the bed and began my search for far-flung garments.

'Don't go yet. We have all night. Anyway, she's not coming till next week.'

'I've got to get back to Max. Last thing he needs is a strung-out mother.'

'Are you pissed off with me?'

Hmm, I wonder.

'Stephan, why the hell are you messing with me when you have someone?'

'I should have told you.'

Snapping, I forwent being cool and pretending it didn't matter.

'Why, Stephan? Does it bolster your ego? Make you feel like the big man? Have you no respect for your partner?'

'We have an open relationship.'

'Yeah, but what about me? You knew I liked you, all you had to say was . . . oh what's the point.'

His answer was to reach out as I was pulling on my jeans and begin stroking my face, which made me want to puke.

'Thanks for the fuck, Stephan.'

Yeah, I got it, real bad. Went home and blasphemed at the Lord.

A MID-MORNING INTERLUDE

SCARFACE: You OK?

UTTER NUTTER: Yeah. Why?

SCARFACE: You're wearing your sunglasses inside.

UTTER NUTTER: Is there a law against it?

SCARFACE: Eh . . . no. I just thought maybe you got into another fight.

UTTER NUTTER: No. But hey, thanks for asking.

SCARFACE: Sure? You're not your usual chirpy self.

UTTER NUTTER: Where's Caligula today?

SCARFACE (*spluttering on some coffee*): Sorry?

UTTER NUTTER (*biting her tongue*): No, I'm sorry, I shouldn't have said that. Sorry, breakfast's on the house.

That day I fought with three customers, short-changed two, broke a plate and took down five wrong orders.

CHERRY ON THE CAKE

This coincided with my father's departure. It was time for him to return, pick up the pieces of his life, and just when we'd got used to his presence. For sure Max would badly miss his grandpa, but I too was dreading living in an adult-empty flat, never mind the prospect of no more free babysitting.

On the eve on his return, we sat round the kitchen table sinking a bottle of red. Our mood was somewhat maudlin. He knew damn well something had happened between Stephan and I. When he'd asked how our date had gone, I'd merely replied, 'It went.'

Still sore and smarting, I'd no desire to see Stephan again. Besides he'd be gone in thirteen days and counting. My disappointment was intense. As far as I was concerned he ceased to exist.

'I'm going to miss Max.'

'He's going to miss you.'

My father had softened the blow with a bag of presents that he'd left at the end of Max's bed. Rising slowly out his chair, he came to kiss me on the top of my head.

'Look, Issy, I know things haven't been easy for you . . . so.'

He delved into his pocket and handed me an envelope.

'Thanks, Dad. You didn't have to.'

'I know. I wanted to.'

Opening the envelope I expected a cheque but my father surprised me with a piece of paper signed by Maria allowing me twenty prepaid babysitting sessions.

'Jesus, Dad, this is brilliant.'

My eyes began to water. It was one of the most thoughtful things my father had ever done.

'How's your mum?' he asked, changing the subject before sentimentality took over.

'Good.'

'Is she still with Randy?'

'His name is Wally.'

'Wally – does he live up to his name?'

'Don't even think of going after Mum again.'

'Issy, please.'

'Don't you remember all the fights?'

'What fights? We were too young to settle down, that was all.'

'You were at each other day and night.'

Damn, but I'd even miss our bickering.

'Dad . . .'

Strange how pauses in conversation are so much more loaded then what is actually said.

'I know,' he answered, 'Don't worry, kid, it will be all right.'

GLUTTON FOR PUNISHMENT

So finally they realised just what a brilliant Honey I was. How they'd actually managed to survive without me, for near on a month, was beyond my reckoning. There was a message to call the Trap and I dialled back, eager to indulge in some ego-massaging,

'Hey, Fiona, it's Issy.'

'Hi, how's your new career taking off?'

'Brilliant, fantastic, everything's –'

'Glad to hear it. We've had good news. Betty dropped her case and business has really picked up. It's suddenly gone crazy.'

'Oh, really?'

'We're run off our feet.'

'I see, so I suppose you think you can just call me up and offer me my job back?'

'Actually, no. We were wondering where the key to the clothes cabinet was. Can't seem to find it anywhere.'

'The key? What about my job?'

'We'll keep you in mind.'

'In mind?'

'So the key – you didn't by any chance take it, accidentally?'

'I want my job back, Fiona.'

'Sorry, Issy, it's gone.'

'What do you mean gone?'

'We've got a replacement.'

'What do you mean replacement?'
'Someone new.'

GOD, WHAT GIVES UP THERE?

Why is it that sometimes you have to shout to be heard?
Take the bank, for example, Say there's a problem and
you go in like a normal person explaining in quiet calm
tones what needs to be done, their usual response is to
ignore you. Whereas, if you make a fuss, start barking
your head off and let your child run riot they will soon
enough pull their finger out of their arses and address
the problem.

So, my Lord, can you hear me or should I adjust the
volume?

Sometimes I reckon you're playing with my emotions.
Bottom line is I need a sign or something to indicate that
I'm not a complete loser.

Thanks,
Issy.

THE SIGN CAME VIA STEPHAN

'Issy . . .'
'Stephan . . .'
Funny how pauses are so much more . . .
Max was asleep when he came knocking.
'I need to speak to you. Can I come in?'

I could do cool courtesy, especially seeing as I'd flushed him from my system (hey, the guy was a shit – boom boom). I opened the door, led him inside.

'I'm sorry about what happened between us.'

He was awkward and hesitant.

'I . . . well, I wanted to say thanks for your help and –'

I was cold and abrupt.

'Where's Katy?'

'At the apartment – we leave tomorrow.'

'Great.'

'And I wanted to tell you, well, it's quite incredible really.'

'Have you sold the flat?'

'Yeah, to a really nice –'

Contender No. 1, Contender No. 1, please let it be Contender No. 1.

'A really sweet couple called the –'

'The Finklesteins!'

I knew it. I goddamn knew it.

I'm jinxed, I swear. I have what is officially known as the Brodsky Touch. Opposite of Midas, in that whatever I touch turns to shit.

'No, it's a young couple – Issy, can I sit down.'

'Oh excuse my inhospitality. Suppose a glass of wine wouldn't go amiss?'

He failed to decode my hint of sarcasm.

'That would be lovely, thanks.'

I poured, we sat, he spoke, I listened.

THE JEWELLER, THE THIEF, HIS WIFE AND A HONEY

There was once a Honey (me), who discovered a severed finger in her garden. OK, so it was Max who actually found it but it was the Honey (me), who brought it to the attention of the police. Not the actual finger, you understand, as unfortunately and through no fault of her own she lost it; perhaps not the best thing to have occurred, but at the time she was under a lot of pressure. A single mother, say no more.

One evening whilst out working, the Honey (me) happened upon a gent of advanced years and some befuddlement, who mistook her for an escort and made her cry. ('Boo hoo hoo, nobody loves me, I'm so alone, life's shit.') Meanwhile in another part of town, a fat detective was busy putting together the pieces of a somewhat strange burglary. A deceased woman had been found in her apartment, missing her little finger and all her jewellery. Soon after the detective met the Honey, and on one occasion, arrived at her door accompanied by the son of the deceased woman. The Honey took a liking to this man and sadly wasted much of the winter mooning over him. As for the elderly gent, Joel Finklestein, he and his wife Gladys spent their winter abroad in the sunny climes of Florida. They did so every year, leaving their jewellery business in the capable hands of their son-in-law, David.

One day a dastardly thief entered the shop, carrying on his person a bag of jewels. The jewels, he claimed, belonged to an elderly aunt who had passed away. He upturned the bag and the jewellery, a selection of necklaces, bracelets, brooches, ear-rings and rings, tumbled out on to the glass counter top. The thief was after a quick cash sale, and offered the lot for five thousand pounds. A bargain, for the real worth of the jewels ran into tens of thousands. Nice pieces, surmised the jeweller's son-in-law, though definitely not kosher. David feigned interest but in the end declined the offer. Taking affront, the thief gathered up the jewels and left.

Later that very day, whilst hoovering before shutting up shop, David came across a small ring, by the side of the counter. A simple silver band with a tiny encrusted emerald and the letters SB engraved on the back. In truth of little value, bar sentiment. It must have slid off the glass top when the thief had laid out his wares. David put it to one side and that was how Joel Finklestein came upon it on his return.

But the story does not end there. The Finklesteins, having lived in a four-bedroom detached house all their lives, decided in Florida that now was a good time to downsize and came to view an apartment in Antrim Road. By fortuitous good timing the Honey (me) was at the apartment, and though initially embarrassed to encounter the Finklesteins, it was she (me) who informed them of the sad demise of Sarah Bloch. Indeed the information given impressed itself upon Joel Finklestein and he wondered if perhaps the ring belonged to the deceased. So it was that by the forces of serendipity and coincidence, all linked by the Honey (me, the centrifugal force of this story), that the ring found its way home.

'Yes, Jeremy that's right. You don't mind me calling you Jeremy?'

Beneath the scorching studio lights I prayed my sweat stains wouldn't show. Prime-time TV; I mean who'd have thought? Maybe a five-minute slot with Richard and Judy, but this was beyond even my expectations. Jeremy Paxman. I think it's the large sloping nose that provides the pow-wow factor. A hint of what lies below? Alas I would never find out.

'And now we have in the studio, Issy Brodsky . . .'

A human interest story that had a nice ring to it. (Painful, hey?) OK, so I didn't exactly make it on to *Newsnight*, but the story spread like, well, spread, and before long I was munching on the leaf-edge of local celebrity.

Bambuss called, offering advice on how to survive the limelight, and saying should he be required he was more than willing to contribute.

'Thanks, but no thanks. I think I can handle it myself, Detective.'

'Be careful what you say. Journalists have a knack for twisting the truth.'

I promised to bear it in mind and enquired after his recent all-over body wax. Maria had sought and taken my advice on finding him an unusual gift for his birthday.

'Yes, Miss Brodsky, I have you to thank for my afternoon of torture.'

'A pleasure,' I assured him.

Besides, on Maria's last visit she'd confided, 'He like a new man, a smooth operator.'

Oh how my head swelled, and as I am so superficial, I got my legs waxed and even had a facial. As I said to Nadia, 'It's not all it's cracked up to be. The pressure to look good is unbelievable.'

'Issy, you've been interviewed on two local radio shows.'

'Tip of the iceberg, my good friend. How do I look?'

'Fine.'

'Only fine?'

The story had been covered, *sans* photo, in the *Antiques Gazette*, *Ham and High* and *Camden New Journal*. But now the big time beckoned and Max and I were expected at the Finklesteins' to be zapped for the *Jewish Chronicle*.

Nads generously offered to drop me and Max down at their house on Carlton Avenue, no doubt hoping to get her face in the picture too. So I decided to take the bus and we ended up arriving half an hour late.

'What's kept you?' Gladys shrieked with relief, ushering us into her grand home. She was obviously house-proud: most of the furniture was covered in plastic.

'So much easier to keep clean,' she silently mouthed.

There was even a clear plastic runner, which we were instructed to walk along in order to preserve the underfoot sea of beige, which, as if on cue, Max managed to destroy, by spilling his berry juice.

Gladys's face contorted in visible agony, in sharp contrast to her empty proclamation, 'Don't worry about it – these things happen!'

I offered to clean up.

'Under the sink you'll find all you need.'

Joel wanted to know why such a lovely girl as I wasn't married.

'The boychik needs a brother or a sister.'

'First opportunity I get, Mr F, I'll be on the case.'

Meantime Gladys had grabbed either side of Max's face and was tugging gently at his pinched-cheek flesh.

'Get off me,' he shouted at her.

'Not until you give me a kiss,' she demanded.

'Yeughh yuck,' squealed Max, and he ran for his life.

The photographer was eager to get going, so while I mopped up, he began snapping.

THE RESULT?

A double-page spread with a creepy picture of Gladys in a suggestive pose reclining on her chaise longue, Joel standing uncomfortably by her side, and then a smaller photo of Max and my forehead. Goddamnit, but I was usurped by my own son taking centre stage and thwarting my special moment by masking eighty-five per cent of my face with his.

THE ART OF SOCIAL HARA-KIRI

My honour was positively impugned. Nadia howled with laughter, and Silvio decided to blow up the picture and stick it on the café wall, with 'Issy's Moment of Fame' scrawled beneath. Served me right, I suppose, for having obnoxiously boasted about it to all and sundry.

JUST THE WAY IT IS

On the night Stephan came to say goodbye and humbly apologise for misleading me, he reminded me of the wooden box I'd found in Sarah's apartment.

The box! I'd totally forgotten about it.

Where the hell had I put it?

Frantically, I scoured the apartment, finally found it at the bottom of one of Max's baskets of toys.

'Put there for safe-keeping,' I glibly assured Stephan, handing it over to him.

'Sure, and well, thanks, Issy – this is for you.'

We exchanged boxes, a big for a little one.

Stephan was to surprise me once more, though this time it was rather touching.

See . . . as for the ring –

It lay inside the box he gave me.

And now I wear it on my little finger.

My left-hand pinkie.

THE LADY IN THE PARK (OR WHAT GOES AROUND COMES AROUND)

Way back when, in the mists of my memory, I vaguely recall an afternoon with Max, feeding the ducks and geese in Regent's Park. Max was two and I merely existing, being sleep-deprived and functioning on auto-pilot. It was fierce cold, the middle of winter, and wrapped up warm, we were swarmed by feathered friends glad of the crumbs we scattered. Hundreds clucked at our feet and we soon ran out of stale bread.

'What a beautiful boy,' smiled an old woman, offering Max a large chunk of bread.

Max continued to feed the ducks and we began chatting. I was so glad of the company, too much time spent on my own with Max, and we ended up in the lakeside café nattering about who knows what over tea and scones.

When Max saw the ring, he said, 'Like the lady in the park.'

In the café my little magpie Max had taken a shine to one of the rings on her fingers.

She'd let him play with it.

I'm almost certain.

But this was a long time ago and perhaps my memory was teasing me.

ON THE UP AND UP

I put my father's generous present to good use and enrolled in a stand-up comedy course at the Amused Moose. Joe the comedian suggested I gave it whirl. Thus I found myself up at the Enterprise of a Saturday afternoon, making a right tit of myself, while Maria sat for Max. Hadn't had so much fun in an age – jeez, when I think of all that money wasted on counselling.

This coincided with my promotion at the café, to 'general manager'. I'd persuaded Silvio to amend my status, arguing it would undeniably raise my morale and thus I would work harder.

'You drive a hard bargain, Issy, but no more wage increases.'

Having recently received one, I didn't mind.

'Oh and Silvio, can I wear a "general manager" badge, just so everyone knows?'

'You buy it, wear whatever you want.'

I had Silvio in the palm of my hand, having implemented certain changes in the café, which brought the punters rolling in. It was easy, and so damn obvious. I set up a mums' morning club, so that full-timers could while away a couple of hours in a kid-friendly environment. All it took was a basket of toys in the corner and the ingenious invention of Fun Froth. Yep, while Mummy was sipping her mid-morning coffee, offspring was offered a cup of milk froth with hundreds and thousands scattered on top, not to mention a special kiddies' menu, including puréed veg for the teeny-tinies. For the mums, lots of low, low-calorific but tasty guilt-free dishes.

Plus, and as I am one to boast, our kid-friendly policy operated during the café's usually dead hours, i.e. ten–twelve and three–five.

Word spread and soon enough they were coming in from far and wide. 'Oh, what a cutie,' I'd insincerely coo about a thousand times a day at wee blighters, nay, savages, who ran amok, leaving grubby paw-prints all over the place and making an unholy mess. But as Fiona once remarked, 'Business is business.'

WELL I NEVER

She showed up in a rather fetching Nicole Farhi linen number.

'Issy, can I have a word.' Fiona hollered above a screeching brat.

'Give me a minute,' I pleaded, surprised to see her,

then turned to the offensive tyke and said, 'Oi, Beyoncé, zip it.'

She got the message and pranced back to her yummy mummy.

'Nice badge,' remarked Fiona.

'Thanks. So what can I get you?'

'I have interesting news. Can we talk?'

Long overdue a break, and notwithstanding the fact I was now general manager, I got one of our recent recruits, an aspiring actress, to hold the fort while Fiona and I skipped over the road, to a quieter café.

BOB A JOB

After all, he had lost me mine.

Once seated comfortably, Fiona began to enlighten me on the Bob Thornton case, and the current state of his marriage.

'Fiona, do I really want to hear this?'

'Yes,' she replied, 'I think you do.'

Bob Thornton and his wife had finally resolved the situation through the simple technique of communication. A procedure that if it should ever catch on would put the Honey Trap out of business pronto.

But back to the saga. Bob's wife had kept a steady check on all his extra-curricular Internet activity, which included membership of a heap of porn sites, dating chat rooms, etc. She was confused to say the least as Bob was a man who rarely veered off the missionary position. Yes, to all intents and purposes, he was the perfect husband, but for this unusual behaviour. She couldn't make head nor tail of it and had then contacted the Trap hoping to obtain some hard evidence of marital transgression. At the same time Bob began acting cagey with her, suspicious of her every move, till finally, after skirting round the issue for an age, he confronted her.

'He confronted her?'

I was baffled.

'He noticed payments made to net sites on his visa bill, to porn sites, and thought she was the culprit.'

'Yeah right, Fiona. He was playing mind games, aware that she had found him out. Slime ball just wanted to pass the buck, blame her.'

'Apparently not. In the end it turned out that their teenage son was the culprit and had been using Bob's name and visa card.'

'The son!'

FLASHBACK TO . . .

The youngster escorted from the bar on the night I went to meet Bob, the group of adolescents at the gig with the seductive chat-up line of, 'Me mate wants to cop off with you.'

It did make sense.

'So are you saying. I didn't fuck Bob?'

'Suffering delusions, it would seem. An attention-seeking exercise that cost you your job. Issy, you caused us a lot of trouble.'

'But we did.'

'No, you didn't.'

'Did.'

Fiona lowered her eyelids and sanctimoniously remarked, 'If I remember correctly you were very frustrated at the time.'

'Fiona, I am not delusional.'

'Be that as it may –'

'Fiona, Bob is a bona fide head-messer. He's a shrink. Look, he's obviously got his wife in a state of derangement.'

'Bob Thornton is a secondary-school teacher.'

'Oh . . .'

The news took a few moments to sink in. So Bob wasn't Bob, as in not the person I thought he was, as in, a complete stranger.

Chrissakes, all the needless worry and grief I'd suffered. The saddest thing was, we'd had a laugh together that night. He was nice, gave me his number, asked me to call him. There we were, two lonely souls randomly seeking out some human comfort.

'Shite, what a waste.'

'Waste?'

'Maybe I could trace him.'

'Who?'

'The other Bob.'

'Well, now that's cleared up, fancy a piece of cake?'

'Another? Jeez, Fiona, hasn't anyone yet mentioned the hip-lip factor?'

And the next thing I knew her face fell. Guess I must have hit a raw nerve. Her eyes welled up and she began blubbing.

'It's the hormones,' she snivelled, 'I can't bear all this effusive emotion.'

'Welcome to the real world of womanhood.'

'I'm taking a drug that replicates the female menstrual cycle. It's horrendous – one minute I'm snapping, next I'm weeping, then there's the water retention. Why didn't anyone tell me it would be like this?'

'Would you have listened?'

'Maybe,' she quietly whimpered, dabbing a tissue

at the corners of her mascara-run eyes.

'Well, there are positives to being a woman.'

'Like what?'

'Mmm, let's see. The ability to bring another being into the world. For all its negatives, being a mother is, well, the very core of what it is to be a female.'

'That's so cruel, Issy.'

Sure it was, but I couldn't resist.

'OK, what about all the male attention we get? Though to be honest it only lasts till you're about thirty. Yeah, hit thirty, the lines start coming, the hair starts turning grey and before you know it you're up Blind Alley, way past your sell-by-date and ignored by all mankind. Sure, who am I to tell you, Fiona?'

Her eyes spouted a fresh batch of tears.

'Issy, it took me twenty minutes to reverse-park this morning.'

THEN TWO LEMON TARTS LATER . . .

Her mood swang back and she was happy as, pie. (Ouch, but I think I'm perfecting the art of naff gags.)

Blushing, Fiona excused her little outburst of emotion and proceeded to inform me that my replacement had turned out to be a total psycho. A deeply insecure woman who ended up frightening off all her dicks by acting like some emotional cripple on acid.

'The upshot being, Issy, that now the Bob file is closed, we'd like you to –'

'Fiona, I get the gist. But before I consider anything, it would be really nice if Trisha was to call me.'

I be the smuggest of all.

'Sorry, what was that, Trisha? I can't hear you.'

Monday afternoon, a fine summer day. Max and I had just reached the top of Primrose Hill. London lay at our feet, and as we peered into the distance, the future was looking good. And that's when Trisha's call came through.

'So as I said, we were hoping you'd consider coming to work for us again.'

Goddamn, the background silence was deafening.

'One more time, Trisha, but with feeling.'

'Would you like your job back?'

Squirm, lady, squirm.

'My job back? You're offering me my job back?'

'Yes.'

'As in, work for the Honey Trap?'

'Yes, Issy.'

'And just so we get things straight, what exactly are the working conditions and pay?'

'Same as before!'

'Hmm, what about a sweetener?'

'We've really missed you.'

'Not tempting enough.'

'OK, how does a five per cent rise sound?'

'Pitiful.'

'Ten per cent.'

'Better.'

'So?'

'I'll give the offer due consideration and get back to you in a couple of days. How's that?'

'Fine, but don't leave it too long.'

Oh, but it does feel good to be wanted. Besides which,

I really wasn't sure how long I could bear another morning of having to deal with a troop of spoilt, demanding café brats, and I'm talking here about the mothers.

Turning to Max, I joyfully exclaimed, 'Maxy, I have a strange feeling.'

'What, Mum?'

'That things can only get better. OK, kid, race you to the bottom of the hill.'

Off we sprinted and this time I didn't let him win.

REVIEWING THE SITUATION

Friday night and I was on a slow saunter home from visiting comedian Joe and Dina, now the proud parents of a seven-pound baby girl.

'So are you going to do it?' Joe asked, alluding to the end-of-the-comedy-course, five-minute gig.

I wasn't convinced I had the nerve.

'Nah, it's been fun but –'

'What do you have to lose? Worst-case scenario you fall on your face.'

'Yeah, I'm used to falling.'

'I'll help with your material.'

'Promise?'

Me, a stand-up comic? Hell, I'd give it a go, nothing ventured . . . I let my mind spin different scenarios as I turned the corner into my street. In this cloistered world of my own, I bathed in the sound of applause, laughter and adulation. Then, but steps away from the apartment, a guy suddenly stumbled out of the shadows, grabbed my shoulder and stopped me in my tracks.

The Brodsky touch!

Just when I was feeling confident again, only to turn

the corner and be mugged. Hey, and there's a joke in there somewhere.

So this was it then, to be assaulted but seconds from safety. My lower jaw dropped open, ready to emit a screech, but nothing came out. My fight or flee mechanism failed to kick in and I froze on the spot, as an icy fear enveloped me.

Christ, and destined to happen on this of all nights. I mean how did the geezer know I was carrying my wages on me?

'Issy!'

And how did he know my name?

'Issy?'

Phew, it was only the upstairs neighbour, carrying upon his person one too many. He staggered to my side and leant heavily against me.

'Did I scare you?'

'Yeah, fuckwit,' and I gave him a dead arm.

'Ouch, what was that for?'

'For scaring the shite out of me.'

'Sorry, I'm pissed.'

'I noticed.'

We stumbled up the steps to the door and I kept trying to shrug him off. I have a very low tolerance of drunkards of his level. It reminds me of what I must be like. Anyhow, he'd begun rambling inchoate sentences.

'It's over.'

'You OK?'

'Issy, come upstairs with me?'

'Why?'

''Cause,' and he wagged his finger in my face, 'I need to talk.'

'We can talk in the morning. Just make sure you grab the banisters on your way up.'

I turned towards my apartment ready with the keys to let myself in.

'She's dumped me.'

'Who?'

'My girlfriend.'

'Oh . . . Congratulations, that's fantastic.'

He slumped down on the bottom stair.

'We had a huge fight.'

He paused, having lost his train of thought.

'Don't worry, she'll be back.'

'Not sure I want her back.' He staggered to an upright position. 'Thanks for listening,' then began a slow climb up the stairs.

'You could do better than her. Believe me, you're well out of it.'

He stumbled and fell, yeah, he was well out of it.

Maria was waiting inside, with a mug of tea at the ready.

'I heard you with someone, thought maybe a new boyfriend?'

'My upstairs neighbour.'

'Oh, anything you want to tell me?'

'No.'

'Really?'

'Yeah, actually, there is something.' I told her about the upcoming gig. 'So I'm depending on you for next week, OK?'

'You really gonna do it?'

'Yeah, why? Do you think maybe I'm crazy?'

'No, is good idea, Issy. I know you can do it.'

'And don't tell anyone, OK?'

'Why?'

'Just don't, it may well be, probably will be, the most mortifying evening in my life.'

Lying in bed, my belly already turbulent, I imagined standing up at the microphone attempting to make people laugh. The prospect was wholly daunting. Joe, true to his word, had helped me during the week with my material.

'Remember, timing and delivery. You'll be fine, Issy.'

'You a hundred per cent certain?'

'Ninety-nine per cent.'

God, it's that one per cent of doubt. It gets me every time.

The intervening days had sped by. I'd called the Trap and was duly reinstated, whey hey, and then relinquished my general manager's badge.

Good old Silvio understood.

'No problem, is for best. I see your heart not in it.'

He was right, the novelty of waitressing had worn thin and I'd been slacking the last while. My upstairs neighbour had recovered from his hangover, but, feeling sorry for himself, moped around the café all week. I took pity on him and was nice for a change.

My head sank back on the pillows, my mind continuing to race. Why did I put myself in such impossible situations? I clasped my hands tight to my chest, 'Dear God,' I moaned aloud.

Yeah, time for a spot of praying.

Dear God,

I am lying here, looking up at the cracks in my bedroom ceiling – guess I'm going to have to redecorate soon. God, you wanna know something? For once I'm truly happy with my lot. Been thinking about recent events, about Sarah and how terrifying it is to be so vulnerable and alone. It's made me realise just how much we need each other. How one can exist in a bubble of independence for only so long.

This evening, when Max was in the toilet, I was struck by the depth of feeling I have for him.

'Max,' I said, 'you're the most amazing boy in the whole wide world and I love you so much it hurts.'

His reply?

'Do you want a plaster?' And then offered me up his butt to wipe.

Then to top it off he asked, 'Mum, what's love?'

And without thinking I said, 'Love, my boy, is being able to laugh through the shit times.'

Listen to me, are you cringing out up there? Oh, I dunno but I just feel feather-light, that anything is possible. I'm ready to give – do you know what I mean? Course you do.

Anyway, I'm doing this gig later today, so wish me luck 'cause . . .

HERE GOES EVERYTHING – THE DAY OF THE GIG

12 p.m. Illicitly scoffing a chocolate croissant, crouched beneath the counter, when Silvio caught me and then charged me full price. Bastard.

1.30 p.m. Neighbour called by with a good-luck card saying, 'Please stop calling me neighbour and/or Scarface. I have a name.' He left the card unsigned. Hilarious, not.

2.15 p.m. Methodically wiping down tables, I was suddenly hit with a rush of dread, ran to the toilet and puked.

3 p.m. Picked up Max from nursery. His teacher pulled me aside and, in a concerned voice, told me Max had got into a fight with an older child. Apparently Max had bragged to him that I was a spy and this kid, along with others, began taunting Max and calling him a liar. Irate, to say the least, I made her and the remaining children apologise on the spot for doubting his veracity. Then the pair of us went to Marine Ices and gorged ourselves on triple cones.

4 p.m. At the playground when Freddie phoned, wondering where I was, having called by the café. He announced he was getting married to the waiter, who happened to be a brain-surgeon student, and would like to spend more time with Max, as they might choose to adopt in the future.

5.30 p.m. At home, I fixed Max his tea and bathed him.

6.30 p.m. Maria called and said she wasn't able to babysit.

6.31 p.m. 'What do you mean? I was depending on you. I have a gig, my first ever gig. This is a huge deal for me. Don't you have any idea how much work I've put into this? Jesus, Maria.'

My otherwise cool demeanour evaporated and I totally lost it.

'I so sorry, I swear, is impossible to come.'

'Why? Why? Why?'

'I in Paris with Bambuss. He whisk me away, say we going to Brighton and be back by five. I'm so very sorry. Issy, you hate me?'

'Very much, Maria.'

This I said coldly, quietly, then slammed down the receiver.

What now, think, think, was there anyone else I could call last minute to babysit?

6.45 p.m. Called Nadia – engaged.

Called Freddie – engaged, as in he and lover boy were otherwise engaged.

Called Fiona – on a date with a sailor she'd just met.

Called Silvio – in the semi-finals of a bowls competition.

Called Joy – in New Mexico living with an amazing guy and three months pregnant.

Called Trisha, as a last resort – she would if she could, but unfortunately was on a mission.

Called Nadia again – still engaged.

Called Joe – he said no and why not bring Max along.

Was he crazy? Had he no idea that after a certain hour children are lethal? It just wasn't possible. No, there was no way.

Called the lovely Finklesteins – no, there was no way. After having three of their own and six grand-kids, Gladys duly informed me, 'We've suffered enough already.'

My neighbour! Bingo. Why didn't I think of him before, my lovely, kind-hearted, generous, child-loving neighbour was – was out.

I knocked, I hollered, I looked out on to the road and his car wasn't in its usual parking space.

8 p.m. I sat on the sofa cuddling Max, trying to coax him out of watching his *Transformers* video.

'Come on, it'll be a laugh, it's comedy.'

'No, I want to watch my video.'

'Oh what's the point.'

I resigned myself to staying in. Besides, who was I kidding? It was a fancy, a mere daydream.

What was I thinking anyway, that I was young, free and single?

I crossed the room to draw the string on my new wood-slat blinds, a recent purchase – when who should appear right in front of me, only Mrs O', what the hell was her name again? Eh . . . eh, it began with L . . .

I ran to the main door, yanked it open and blared at her as she scuttled down the road.

'Oi, Mrs –' It was on the tip of my tongue. 'Mrs Lynch.'

My voice resonating from here to kingdom come.

'Course I will. Sure, it's not a bother. It'll be a pleasure. Where is the little mite?'

'Omigod you don't know how appreciative I am.'

I rose up and brushed down my dusty street-soiled knees.

8.30 p.m. Already expected at the club, but in the shower.

Max and Mrs Lynch playing snakes and ladders in the front room.

8.45 p.m. Still damp, pulled on my clothes.

8.46 p.m. Out of the house and I ran, hell for leather, all the way there. I would do it. I could do it.

'They're not going to get me, they're not going to get me . . .'

9.01 p.m. Arrived, drenched in sweat, and realised my T-shirt was on inside out.

Joe was at the door of the bar.

'You made it, brilliant, we got a big house inside.'

Oh Christ, head swirling with panic. Not sure I could do it now. Hey, it was only five minutes, five whole minutes, a friggin' lifetime, 300 seconds of . . . No, I could do it.

'You're first up, Issy. Let's go.'

9.05 p.m. The place was packed. OK, so it only seated twenty people but that was twenty too many people to humiliate myself in front of. I stayed at the rear – Joe was on stage, warming the crowd up. Focus, girl, keep it concentrated.

And then . . . I heard my name.

OK, I could do it. I could do it.

Up I strode, side-glancing the audience. Oh Sweet Jesus, 'cause there they all were, Bambuss and Maria, Nadia, Fiona, Trisha, my neighbour, the Finklesteins, Silvio, even goddamned Freddie and his beau.

Here goes everything.

I . . .

I . . .

I took a deep breath and –

BOMBED

Goddamnit. It was excruciating, it was –

'Not as bad as all that,' my neighbour lied.

'Really?'

'The "Bohemian Rhapsody" scene was funny.'

Don't ask – I'd done it as a last resort, pulled it from my subconscious, desperate to get a reaction from the audience.

My neighbour and I trudged home in silence.

'Sorry if I wasted your evening,' I mumbled as we reached the front door.

'You didn't.'

Aw shucks, there he was doing his utmost to raise my spirits.

'Any news from your ex?'

'No.'

'Oh well. So what was the argument about?'

'You.'

'Me?'

'She reckons I fancy you and I'm in denial.'

'Ha!'

'And that applies to you too.'

'As if.'

'So, Ms Brodsky, can I kiss you?'

OK, OK, I succumbed and, in the cringe-inducing spirit of my stand-up, will always recall that evening as the night I died and went to –

A NOTE ON THE AUTHOR

Thea Wolff claims to be twenty-one but is lying. Born in Dublin, she's been living in London long enough to know better. And yes, she is a single mother.

A NOTE ON THE TYPE

The text of this book is set in Linotype Sabon, named after the type founder, Jacques Sabon. It was designed by Jan Tschichold and jointly developed by Linotype, Monotype, and Stempel, in response to a need for a typeface to be available in identical form for mechanical hot metal composition and hand composition using foundry type. Tschichold based his design for Sabon roman on a font engraved by Garamond, and Sabon italic on a font by Granjon. It was first used in 1966 and has proved an enduring modern classic.